**"Bastard," the man muttered,
glaring at Longarm.**

"That's twice," Longarm said, remembering an old
joke.

"Bastard."

Third time, Longarm thought with a suppressed sigh.
It seemed quite enough.

Longarm looked at the rest of the silent, uncomfortable men standing at the bar. "Do you know what you
boys need in this town?" he asked them. "A public
sanitation department"—he looked directly at Ez—
"to haul shit away when it's piled so high."

Ez drew back and flung his empty glass at Longarm's
face. He followed the thrown missile with a ponderous
lunge.

Time for a little exercise, Longarm thought.

Also in the LONGARM series
from Jove

TABOR EVANS

LONGARM

AND THE STAGECOACH BANDITS

A JOVE BOOK

LONGARM AND THE STAGECOACH BANDITS

A Jove Book / published by arrangement with
the author

PRINTING HISTORY
Jove edition / December 1985

ISBN: 0-515-08422-0

Jove books are published by The Berkley Publishing Group,
200 Madison Avenue, New York, N.Y. 10016. The words
"A JOVE BOOK" and the "J" with sunburst are trademarks
belonging to Jove Publications, Inc.

PRINTED IN THE UNITED STATES OF AMERICA

Chapter 1

Longarm nodded to Henry, United States Marshal Billy Vail's meticulous and sometimes rather priggish clerk, and deliberately dropped his Stetson onto a vacant chair in the outer office, ignoring the hat rack only a few paces away.

If that annoyed Henry, Longarm thought, well... good. Longarm was in a mood to snap at someone today. Damn near anyone would do.

What really bothered Deputy Marshal Custis Long about this morning's foul humor was that there was no good reason for it. Oh, his stomach was a trifle sour from last night's whiskey. He was feeling a bit logy and leaden from lack of sleep after last night's other exertions. But he was used to those things. Normally he could bounce back at the break of day ready for anything. Not this morning. And there was just no good reason for it.

Boredom, he had finally concluded. Sheer, simple boredom.

For the better part of a week he had been keeping himself on call for court appearances to testify in this case or about that past-and-done-with matter.

And courtroom appearances were hardly exciting. For the most part they consisted of sitting on a hard bench in the hallway outside the federal court, waiting for some dumb, damn defense lawyer to call him inside for a few brief minutes of unpleasantness while the lawyer tried to convince a judge or a jury or both that Deputy Long was an asshole and the lawyer's client was as innocent as a babe.

No, Longarm thought, work like that was hardly pleasant, and certainly boring. He was plainly fed up with it.

So this morning he was ready to bite heads off or to pick up a willow switch and go to hunting grizzlies. Any damn thing but what he had been doing all this past week.

Henry's eyebrows went up a notch when he saw Longarm plant his Stetson on the chair. For a change, though, the clerk had the good judgement to take a hard look at Longarm's face and the set of the tall deputy's jaw. Henry ignored the affront and motioned Long into the marshal's office.

"Really?" Longarm asked with a suddenly rising hope.

Henry nodded. "He told me to send you in when you got here."

"Good." Longarm felt his mood improving already.

Something big, he hoped. Something that would get him the hell away from courtrooms and hallways and ignorant lawyers. But preferably something big. Something that would be a challenge. Ideally something that would take him to the high country, away from the heat of the plains. This summer and fall had been exceptionally hot. A venture into the mountains would be welcome. Having to look at those high, cool peaks was frustrating each morning when he had to walk to the federal building.

And he had heard on the grapevine that there was a gang of train robbers at work between Georgetown and Silver City.

Longarm actually grinned as he went into Billy Vail's office. That would involve mail robbery too, most likely. So it would come under federal jurisdiction.

That had to be the assignment Billy wanted to see him about. That one would take him up into the high, timbered, cool mountains. The more he thought about it, the more anxious he was to receive the assignment from Billy and get on his way.

Already he could practically taste the cold, fresh bite of the water from the racing streams up there, smell the freshness of pine-scented mountain air, and feel the crispness of the mornings.

Yes, he thought. For a change Billy was going to hand him just the assignment he wanted.

He presented himself before the pink-cheeked, balding, slightly plump man who was the federal marshal for the Justice Department's Denver district and smiled as he pulled a red morocco-covered chair around and straddled it.

"*Good* morning, Billy."

"Well, aren't you in a good mood today?" Vail greeted him.

"Never better," Longarm said cheerfully.

"I'm glad to hear that, Long. I used to think that court appearances bothered you, but now that I know better I won't be so quick to try and get you out of them."

"Billy! Please." Longarm's face fell, and he came half out of the chair.

"Please give you more court appearances? Sure, Longarm, I'd be glad to."

"Damn it, Billy, you *know* what I meant. You can't put any more of this stuff on me. I'd go 'round the bend. You know I would."

Vail looked at him. The marshal's face split open into a knowing grin.

"You oughtn't to do a thing like that to a man, Billy. You could give a feller heart failure."

"Well," Vail said, "as it happens, I do have an assignment that needs to be taken care of."

"Believe me," Longarm said with feeling, "I'm ready for some field work again. I need it."

Vail plucked a slip of paper from his desk and glanced at it.

"Is that the mail-theft thing, Billy?"

Vail looked mildly surprised. "You've heard of it already?"

"I have. And if there's any doubts at all, Billy, I want you to know that I'm interested in taking it on."

"Volunteering, Custis? That isn't like you."

"Damn it, Billy, a week of sitting on my butt getting numb from hard benches and harder heads isn't like me either. So if it comes down to that, yeah, I'm interested enough to say you could call me a volunteer for this one."

"My oh my, Longarm. You do surprise me this morning. I thought for sure you'd want to beg off this case on some pretext or another."

"Not me," Longarm said eagerly.

"I really thought you would be wanting something more exciting for your next assignment."

4

"Mail theft, Billy. That's a serious offense, you know."

"And you would really like to handle it?"

"Absolutely," Longarm assured him.

Vail smiled. "Very well then, Deputy. The Julesburg stage case is all yours."

Longarm's face fell. "Julesburg stage, Billy? They haven't run a Julesburg stage in . . . what . . . ten years? More?"

The marshal was still smiling.

"Besides, I thought we were talking about the Silver City robberies."

"Oh, Dutch and Smiley are already assigned to that matter," Vail said with a joy he no longer bothered to hide. He leaned back in his chair and folded his hands across his belly. "You were busy in court when that one came up, you know."

"But—"

"I know everyone will feel better knowing you are on this case, Longarm."

"But the Overland Company hasn't run a stage out of Julesburg since the railroad came down," Longarm protested.

"I never said anything about the Overland Company, Custis. Now did I?" Vail grinned.

"I thought . . ." Longarm began.

"Did you now? Really, Custis, all I know is that I heard you volunteer for this assignment. I did hear that, didn't I?"

"Yes, but—"

"Of course, I suppose I could put someone else on it. Someone with less experience. That would free you to do important things like serve warrants. And there are some defense attorneys who've been wanting

5

to meet with you for depositions. I had been putting them off, but if you'd rather—"

"No," Longarm said quickly. "No, sir; no way. This Julesburg case sounds pretty good to me. Yes, sir, the more I think about it, Billy, the better it sounds." Longarm pulled a cheroot from his coat pocket and bit off the tip. "Whatever it is."

Billy Vail was still grinning. "I do like it when you report for work with a smile on your face, Custis, and a cheerful, willing attitude toward your work."

"Thanks," Longarm moaned.

This time, damn it, Vail had snookered him. And they both knew it.

Longarm sighed. Julesburg was way the hell and gone out on the plains, just as far as a man could get away from the high, cool mountains and still be in the state of Colorado. That was all right as far as it went, but it was *hot* out there. And barren, and boring, and dusty. And . . . ah, hell, Longarm thought. It was also away from the damned courtrooms and benches and hallways. Anything was better than those benches.

He flickered a match aflame and lighted his cigar. "What the hell, Billy," he said. "Tell me about it."

This should only take a day or three to wind up, Longarm reflected as he packed his gear and ran an oily rag over the barrel of his Winchester. The rifle had picked up some dust sitting there in a corner for the past week. It was good to be going out again.

For a change, the information that had arrived at the marshal's office had been fairly complete.

If he was able to wrap this up quick and clean, Longarm thought, he just might be able to talk Billy into giving him a few days of free time. He could go

6

up to the high country and spend a few days lazing around where the air was cool and the wind free of dust and coal smoke. Maybe go to Georgetown on the pretext of giving Dutch and Smiley a hand, or simply go and do it on his own time. He could recall a lady or two he wouldn't mind looking up if he could find an excuse to head into that part of the country.

In the meantime, all he had to do was pop over to Julesburg and put the irons on whoever was masterminding all these robberies. Judging from the information the Post Office had sent along when they requested help, though, that should not be all that much of a job. The case almost seemed cut and dried.

According to the Julesburg postmaster, the little feeder stage that ran between Julesburg and Holyoke was being robbed pretty regularly, and only when there was something valuable aboard the coach, which pretty well said that the whole thing was an inside job.

So all Deputy Long would have to do would be to step in and rattle the stage-line employees around until the bad apple dropped into the palm of his hand.

Piece of cake, he told himself complacently.

He tried to remember the name of the stage line. It was not the famous Overland Company involved here. They had been put out of business in the Julesburg area years before, when the rails had been completed between Denver and the Union Pacific main line at Julesburg. This was some little outfit Longarm had never heard of before.

Simmons. That was it. Billy had said it was the Simmons Express Company.

Well, he thought, another couple of days and someone in the Simmons Express Company was going to be wearing a new set of bracelets. And Custis Long was going to be asking for some free time.

He snugged the straps of his McClellan saddle, securing the stirrups and girth into a neat, manageable bundle, then slid his Winchester into the scabbard that had been tucked under the jockey and stirrup leathers for travelling.

His carpetbag was already packed. He kept it that way so there would be no delays if he received orders for a quick departure from his boarding-house room on Cherry Street. He looked through the contents, though, to make sure he had a supply of clean clothing, ammunition, telegraph key, and a bottle of Tom Moore rye whiskey. Everything seemed to be in order. Just to make sure, though, he pulled the cork from the bottle of Tom Moore and took a stomach settler. Everything was as it should be.

He replaced the bottle in the bag and got a handful of thin, dark cheroots from his humidor to add to the things in the bag. If he had forgotten those he would have been cursing himself directly.

He picked up his gear and left the room, a tall, lean, brown man wearing a snuff-brown Stetson, a brown tweed coat, tan twill trousers, and stovepipe boots. In addition to the Winchester he carried attached to his saddle he wore a Colt double-action revolver under the left front of his coat, canted for a cross draw that no outlaw had yet been able to match. In addition to his visible weaponry he carried a .41-caliber derringer clipped as a fob on the end of the watch chain that crossed his vest. The little hideout gun had come in handy more than once.

His face was deeply tanned by the rugged, outdoor life he preferred to live. His hair and sweeping, full moustache were brown, and his eyes were the color of gunmetal. His features were firmly molded, softened to some extent by light fans of sun wrinkles at the corners of his eyes.

He was tall, a few inches over six feet, with broad shoulders and a horseman's narrowness of hip. He carried himself with an ease and assurance that had nothing to do with arrogance, everything to do with confidence.

Longarm put his gear onto the front seat of the hack he had kept waiting for him in front of the boarding house, then climbed inside and directed the driver to take him back to the federal building on Colfax. By now Henry should have his travel vouchers ready. As soon as they were in hand he could leave.

Marshal Vail was standing beside Henry's desk when Longarm walked into the office. "Ready to leave, Longarm?"

The marshal's top deputy nodded.

"The P.M. to Julesburg won't be leaving for quite a while yet," Vail said. Henry was shuffling a thin sheaf of papers together, folding them, and stuffing them into an envelope.

"I was thinking about that while I packed," Longarm said. "I don't think I'll be going by way of Julesburg."

Vail gave him a look that might have been amusement. "You're going to Julesburg, but not by the only means of transportation that would take you there. Is that what you're telling me, Longarm?"

Longarm grinned. "Something like that, Billy." He offered no other explanation, but accepted the envelope of vouchers from Henry and tucked them into his inside coat pocket.

"Going to make me ask you, huh?"

9

Longarm shrugged.

"All right, damn it. I'm asking," said Vail.

"What I was thinking, Billy, is that this thing is supposed to be an inside job. So whoever is planning these robberies is likely in the Julesburg stage office. I'd kinda like to get a look at things before I make myself known to those folks, so I thought I'd wander up on them from their blind side. Leave the U.P. alone and take the Burlington line out to Wray, then go up to Holyoke from there and buy myself a ticket north-bound. Get a look at things first, if you see what I mean."

Vail thought about that for a moment, then he grunted.

"Is that your way of telling me you approve?" Longarm asked.

The marshal grunted again.

"You really ought to go into politics, Billy," Longarm suggested. "You'd make a hell of a silver-tongued orator."

"Go away, Longarm. Go get some work done."

"See?" Longarm waved a brief goodbye to Henry and turned to leave.

"Long?"

"Yes, Marshal Vail?"

"The telegraph lines do run between here and Julesburg. Keep that in mind, will you?"

"Don't I always?" Longarm grinned and touched the brim of his Stetson. He slipped out the door and down the hall before Billy Vail could offer any more comments.

Longarm felt good when he got back to the hack. "Burlington depot," he told the driver.

Yes, he thought as he rode. There was nothing like

10

getting back to field duty to make a man feel better. Especially with as easy a case as this one promised to be.

He chuckled and reached for a cheroot. When it was lighted he tipped his hat forward over his eyes and propped his boots on the opposite seat.

Piece of cake, he told himself happily.

Chapter 2

It was already dusk by the time the eastbound Burlington passenger coach reached Wray, just a few miles
short of the Ogallala Trail and the Colorado–Nebraska
line. Longarm left the smoker and walked back along
the platform to claim his gear from the baggage car.

There was not much light left in the sky, but there
was enough to see what there was to see in Wray.
The town lay between the railroad tracks and a thin
line of dark growth—willows, Longarm guessed, although it was too dark for him to tell at that distance—
that would have been the North Fork of the Repub-
lican. The river began somewhere west of Wray and
looped past the town on its way to Nebraska and
eventually to the Kansas and the Missouri. The trickle
of water that flowed here would someday flow past
New Orleans.

The town was not much bigger than the river was
here. A few paces would get you past either one of
them. Lamplight showed along the short stretch of
main street, so Longarm headed in that direction. Wray

was not big enough to boast a Harvey House, so he would have to settle for what he could find.

What he found was a ramshackle hotel that probably could not have had a dozen rooms. It seemed to be the only game in town, though, so Longarm went in and approached the desk.

"Evening, ma'am," he said to the lady behind the counter.

She had been bent low over some papers, with a pencil in her hand. She looked up, a harried, mousy-looking woman with wisps of hair coming undone from her bun.

"Yes?"

"I was hoping you'd have a room, ma'am."

She started to say something but was interrupted by a pair of barefoot boys who came dashing out of a back room. Longarm guessed that the kids were probably five and seven. The smaller of them grabbed for his mother's skirts while the older lunged at him.

"Mama!" the little one shrieked.

The woman hardly bothered to look at them. "Ned, you leave your brother be."

"Yes'm." The boy said it politely enough, but the glare he gave to his smaller brother made Longarm glad that he was not in the little fellow's shoes. Or position. Neither of them was wearing shoes.

"Go on and play now. And mind yourselves. I'll be back to fix your supper in a minute."

"Yes'm."

"Yes, mama."

They turned and were gone as quickly as they had come. "Yes?" the woman asked again.

"About a room, ma'am?"

"Oh, yes." She turned and took a key from one of

14

the boxes. There were ten boxes; Longarm counted them out of idle curiosity and found that his guess of fewer than a dozen had been accurate.

"I only have one room left," she said. "If someone comes in late, you may have to double up."

"I'd rather be by myself," he said.

"So would everyone, mister, but I can't afford to turn away trade, and there's a westbound that comes through about ten o'clock every night. I won't make you no promises. Take it or leave it."

Longarm sighed. "Reckon I'll have to take it."

She sniffed and nodded. She had the only hotel in town and had expected nothing else. "Fifty cents, mister. In advance."

Her attitude was smug and unbending. Longarm began to wonder how she had gotten close enough to anyone to have two children.

"Fifty cents?" he asked.

"In advance." She sniffed again.

"Right." He dug into his pocket and gave her the money. He was tempted to use a government voucher, just to annoy her with the paperwork, but it hardly seemed worth it. Besides, she would probably pad the amount if he did that, and then he would get mad. He paid up and accepted the key she handed him.

"Room nine," she said.

"Where . . . ?" But the boys came racing back. This time the littler one was crying, and his belligerent brother—took after his ma, Longarm concluded— was trying to head him off.

The hell with it, Longarm decided. He would find it himself. If she wanted him to sign a register, she could grab him later. He did not particularly want to stand here and listen to the woman's screaming kids,

15

who were commencing to threaten his eardrums with shouts disputing about which had done what to whom.

"Thanks," he mumbled and turned away.

The room was no better than he would have expected. The furnishings were cheap and few: a bed, a small stand with an almost empty lamp on it, some metal hooks screwed into the wall instead of a wardrobe. There was no chair, and the sheets had not been changed recently enough. The mattress was lumpy and sagged in the middle as deep as a Frazier saddle's seat.

"Welcome to Wray," Longarm said aloud. He set his saddle and carpetbag at the foot of the bed and opened the bag to bring out his bottle of Tom Moore. He had a drink and returned the bottle to the carpetbag. If there was the possibility of having company while he was out, he did not want to leave the liquor in plain sight. One of the few things worse than sleeping with a stranger was sleeping with a strange drunk.

The hotel probably served meals too, but he was not interested in sampling whatever they might have to offer. He pushed his gear beneath the foot of the bed, out of sight, and left to find a halfway decent place to eat.

He found a restaurant in the next block that looked no better than the hotel, but the proprietor, a plump, middle-aged man, was pleasant, and someone back in the kitchen knew how to cook a steak the way a man liked it. Longarm filled up with meat and potatoes and lighted a smoke when he was done. There was something about finishing a good meal that made a cheroot taste all the better.

"That was good," Longarm said as he paid. "Now would you know where I might find something liquid to set things just right?"

16

"If you're looking for something warm and wooly," the restaurant keeper said, "you'll have to go out past the depot the other side of the stockpens. There's a hog ranch over there for those as hasn't got much of a sense o' smell."

"From the stockpens?"

"Nope. The women." The man made a face, then laughed. "But if it's just a drink you want, you won't do any better than next door. The town folk mostly drink at Henry's here. The cowhands go out to Mabel's place."

Longarm nodded. "Reckon I'll pay Henry a visit then. Thanks."

"Come again, mister."

"If you're open for breakfast, I expect I will."

"In that case, tell Henry I sent you. Half price for the first drink."

"Thanks again."

He went out onto the boardwalk and turned left. There was another saloon across the street, but the man had not mentioned it. Longarm decided to accept the local's advice.

The place was busy but not loud. There was no piano or other form of entertainment, just a well-stocked bar that was lined with customers. There was a card game in progress at one of the three tables in the place; the others were empty.

Longarm found a few feet of open bar and moved into it.

"Feller next door suggested I come here," he said when the barkeep stopped in front of him. "If you'd happen to have a bottle of Tom Moore, you'd make my evening complete."

"Bottle or glass, mister?"

"A glass will do."

17

The man poured a small tumbler full of the excellent rye and took only a dime for it. Longarm would have expected to pay that for a shot.

"Thanks."

"You bet." The barman turned to serve someone else.

"New in town?" the man on Longarm's left asked.

"Passing through," Longarm said. He raised the glass and took a swallow from it, enjoying the warmth that spread through his full belly immediately afterward.

"We get a lot of that now," the townsman persisted.

"I'm sure you do."

"Cause of the damned railroad, you know."

"Yes, I'm sure." Longarm set his glass down and wondered if there was another place at the bar open. He had not come here to chat with strangers. All he wanted was a quiet drink and then to go back and go to bed.

"Damn railroad," the town man repeated.

Longarm looked at him for the first time. The man was not especially tall, but he was heavily muscled. He was tanned a rich brown and obviously did his work out in the sun. He had a raggedy-assed moustache that curled down into his mouth and he should have visited a barber, if Wray had a barber, much more recently than he had.

"You work for the damn railroad?" the man demanded.

"No," Longarm said mildly. He took another drink of the rye. It did not taste as good to him this time as the first swallow had. But that was not the fault of the whiskey.

"You look like the kind of bastard would work for

18

a railroad," the townsman said with a glare.

The conversations around them stilled as men up and down the length of the bar became aware of what was happening.

Longarm thought it over for a moment. Perhaps the fool was just drunk, he decided. He took his glass of whiskey and ambled to the nearest empty table, leaving the unhappy town man behind.

"You hear me?" the man asked loudly.

The bartender hurried to him. "Don't get started on that shit again, Ez. You know you just get in trouble every time you do."

The town man, Ez, ignored him. He was staring at Longarm. "You know what the damn railroad does?" he asked.

Longarm paid no attention to him.

"Damn trains come through. Howlin' with their whistles. Hiss and snort. Raise all kinds of hell. Scare shit outa my goats. Every time I hear one of them whistles, man, I know I lost two quarts of milk. Every stinkin' time, I know that. Now what do you have to say about that, mister?"

Longarm looked at him this time but did not bother to give him an answer. The man did not want an answer anyway. He was feeling riled about an old, tired subject, and had found someone new to carp at about it.

"Whyn't you shut up, Ez, an' let the gentleman drink in peace," a drinker at the bar said.

Longarm looked at the man and raised his glass toward him in silent thanks.

"Don't try and tell me what to do, Brownie, or I'll take your damn head off. I done it before, and I can do it again."

The man who had spoken flushed and turned away, embarrassed by the public reminder that he had once been whipped, but not willing to prove that it could not be done a second time.

"Leave be, Ez," the bartender said, "or I'll have to ask you to quit coming here again."

"Up yours," Ez muttered. He turned back toward Longarm. "An' you," he snarled. "You're the kind as thinks he's too good to listen to a poor man's troubles, ain't you?" He tossed back the liquor in the glass he had been holding and glared at Longarm. "Bastard."

"That's twice," Longarm said, remembering an old joke.

"Bastard."

Third time, Longarm thought with a suppressed sigh. It seemed quite enough.

Longarm looked at the rest of the silent, uncomfortable men standing at the bar. "Do you know what you boys need in this town?" he asked them. "A public sanitation department"—he looked directly at Ez—"to haul shit away when it's piled so high."

Ez drew back and flung his empty glass at Longarm's face. He followed the thrown missile with a ponderous lunge.

Time for a little exercise, Longarm thought.

Longarm leaned to his right, sliding off the chair and rising in a single fluid motion. He did not hurry. He did not have to. Ez's senseless, bullying anger had already committed him to both direction and speed. Longarm shifted smoothly aside, out of the way.

The chair Longarm had been sitting on remained, however. Directly in Ez's path.

The townsman crashed into it and fell in a wild

heap of swinging arms and flailing legs. He cursed as he went down.

"Oops," Longarm said with a sardonic grin.

"You son of a bitch." Ez scrambled to his knees and then upright, back onto his feet.

"You know," Longarm said, "you've already made an ass of yourself. Now you're coming close to making me mad." His expression and tone of voice hardened. "I don't think you really want to do that."

"Son of a bitch," Ez accused.

Longarm kept his eyes locked onto Ez, but his words were addressed to the other men in the bar. "I don't figure to be patient much longer with this pile of crap."

"Ez don't look like much," one of them answered, "but he can whup about anybody in Wray." There was an odd note of pride in the man's voice.

"And any railroad-lovin' son of a bitch that passes through," Ez added.

"You got to do it before you can claim it," Longarm said calmly.

Ez brushed his hands together and stood where he was for a moment. His face and thick neck were red, and his breathing came heavier and faster. He was working himself up to it, Longarm thought. Readying himself like a damn bull pawing the ground before it charged. Longarm stood quietly and waited for Ez.

This time when he came it was with no blind rush, though. This time Ez dropped into a crouch and scuttled toward his opponent with his hands extended, ready to grab rather than punch.

Longarm took note of the man's posture, especially with his hands.

Ez was not tall, Longarm saw. He did not have a

21

prizefighter's reach or whipcord build. Instead he was blocky, his arms ropy with thick slabs of muscle, his neck so wide and solid it almost looked as if he had no neck, that his head and shoulders joined without interruption.

He was a grappler, then, Longarm thought. His plan would be to take a grip on the other fellow and close with him, wrap those powerful arms around him, and crush ribs with the force he could apply.

Knowing this, Longarm knew how to handle him.

Ez shuffled closer, hands held at the ready, with the fingers splayed rather than fisted.

Longarm let him come nearer . . . let him come in as close as he wished.

Or almost that near.

As Ez closed on him, Longarm leaned forward. A rock-hard plane of fist jabbed out with the speed of a striking snake to connect with the bridge of Ez's nose once, twice, three times. Then Longarm was darting backward, light and swift on the balls of his feet.

The combination had been quick and seemingly casually delivered, but now Ez was bleeding heavily from his nose, and a swelling began to form under the man's right eye. Longarm was distantly aware of yelling behind him. Someone was taking bets on the outcome of the fight.

Ez stopped and shook his head, flinging droplets of bright blood onto the floor and onto men standing near him. He wiped his nose with the back of his wrist, and his eyes widened when he saw the amount of blood there.

"Bastard," he shouted.

Longarm waited. Again Ez dropped into his wrestler's crouch and shuffled forward, pressing for an opportunity to lay hands on his quarry.

Longarm moved lightly away, bobbing and darting in time to some inner rhythm.

Every time Ez closed on him that left would flick out again to snap Ez's head back and send blood flying.

"You son of a bitch," Ez shouted. "Stand and fight like a man."

Longarm's answer was another jab with his left. But this time, now that Ez was used to the pattern, Longarm did not dance quickly away again. This time he stepped in closer and delivered a whistling right cross that caught Ez flush on the chin.

The local brawler's eyes lost their focus, and his knees sagged. His hands flexed futilely in thin air, unable to find flesh or cloth.

Longarm took a step to the side and flashed the left out again two, three, four times. Ez was as good as done already. He was unsteady on his feet, weaving from side to side.

"Unfair," someone behind Longarm cried. "The son of a bitch's a professional fighter. Jus' look at him."

Ez blinked, and somehow maintained his footing. Again he extended his hands and tried to move in in that low, crouching scuttle. The scrabbling motion reminded Longarm of a crab he had seen once on a beach at Galveston.

"Stand and fight." It came out almost as a plea this time.

Longarm stabbed him with the lightning-quick left twice more and moved to his left, intending to step in and finish it with a final, devastating right.

Someone thrust something—a broom handle, an ankle, Longarm never knew what—between Longarm's feet. He lost his balance for a moment and stumbled.

Ez roared with joy and leaped forward.

One immensely powerful hand closed over Longarm's wrist, and he was drawn forward before he could regain his balance.

"Now," Ez cried.

Longarm threw his elbow but the hard, bony joint missed its intended target over Ez's solar plexus and connected only with bone. Ez grunted in pain but kept his concentration. He pulled Longarm nearer, and his other arm snaked out to wrap around Longarm's back.

Longarm tried to spin and whirl away, but Ez's hold was too powerful to be broken so easily.

Inexorably, like a fish on heavy line, Longarm was reeled in closer and closer until his chest was pressed against Ez's, until they were chin to chin and eye to eye.

He could feel Ez's arms around and behind him, could feel the difference when Ez finally was able to grasp one wrist with his other hand and really begin to apply pressure.

Longarm gasped. Never had he encountered any human force so powerful. Ez had the strength of a machine. And now he had leverage as well. The man's face became even redder, and the sinews and veins along the side of his neck corded and swelled as he bore down with everything he had.

What he had was a killing strength. Once the first rib went the others would follow, and Longarm's chest and upper body would be literally crushed.

Already Longarm could not breathe. He gasped for

air but had no room to draw oxygen into his lungs. His vision began to cloud.

Longarm raised his foot and kicked forward and down, raking the heel of his boot down Ez's shin and onto the top of his foot.

Ez cried out in pain, but his grip never lessened. If anything, the pain and the anger made his hold all the tighter. He arched his back and held Longarm's feet off the ground so he could not do it a second time.

Longarm tried kneeing Ez in the crotch, but the man was too savvy for that. He turned the knee with his thigh and tugged viciously at his imprisoned opponent.

Longarm reached between them in search of his Colt. The choice seemed simple enough: do something quickly or die. He forced his hand between them and grasped the butt of the revolver. Some spectator, probably one who had bet on Ez to win, saw what he was doing and snatched his arm away with a cry of "No fair!"

I'll show you fair, Longarm wanted to tell the bastard, but he did not have any breath left for talking.

He was seeing things through a thick, red fog now. He could not hold out much longer.

He tried again to hurt Ez with the heel of his boot, but the blocky man only lifted him higher, arching himself further backward until Longarm was virtually suspended in the air above him, with their torsos locked into one solid mass.

Longarm tried to raise his arms, tried desperately to break Ez's hold, but the man was too powerful, too experienced.

Longarm groaned. The sound was horrifying to

him. It meant he had lost still more of his scant, precious supply of air. He had not been able to help himself.

His head sagged forward in a sham attempt to convince Ez that Longarm had already passed out so that possibly, just possibly, Ez would release his hold.

Instead, the hint of victory lent Ez more strength than ever, and he clamped his arms around Longarm like a vise with ever-growing strength.

Longarm's head sagged forward until his face was pressed against Ez's, his sweat mixed with Ez's.

Longarm could see nothing. He could still feel. He felt Ez's unkempt moustache against his cheek.

Desperate, able to think of nothing else, Longarm turned his head a fraction of an inch and opened his mouth. He captured the side of Ez's nostril between his teeth and bit down. Hard.

Ez screamed and tried to pull away. Longarm bit with all the strength he had left and ground his teeth together with the fold of Ez's flesh between them.

Ez screamed again and tried to pull his head away from Longarm's. The movement overbalanced him, and they both fell heavily.

Longarm landed on top of Ez. He could hear the breath gush out of the blocky man's chest.

Much better than that, though, Longarm could breathe himself as Ez lost his hold and his arms fell away from Longarm's sides.

The air that Longarm gulped was finer-tasting than any glass of whiskey he had ever had, clearer and fresher than water from a mountain stream.

He rolled away from Ez and grabbed at a table top, pulling himself to his feet while his lungs and chest heaved and pulled at the newly available oxygen. He was greedy for it. And shaken.

Ez was on his feet too, though. He was back into that crouch. Those dangerously powerful hands were extended, fingers flexed and grasping.

Fair, Longarm thought. *I'll show you fair.*

He stepped forward and snapped his leg up, driving the toe of his boot under Ez's chin and lifting the bastard several inches.

He heard bone shatter as Ez's jaw broke, and the man screamed.

"No fair!" a spectator shouted.

Doubled over with pain, still gasping for lack of air to breathe, hair spilling down over his sweaty forehead, and with raw fury now smouldering in his eyes, Longarm turned and fixed a furious glare on the spectator.

The fellow already had his mouth open to speak again. He stopped before the first sound was out of his mouth. He blinked rapidly and began to back away. "I never meant nothin' by it, mister."

"Uh-huh," Longarm grunted.

The spectator turned and beat a hasty retreat out of the saloon.

Longarm found his hat lying on the floor. He picked it up, brushed the underside of the brim free of sawdust, and looked around the room with disgust.

The men in the place were quiet. Over in a corner, someone had produced a list and was paying off bets to those who had put their money on the stranger.

Longarm saw his glass on the floor near where his hat had fallen. It was tipped on its side. The excellent rye it had contained was nothing more than a damp spot now. *Piss on 'em,* Longarm thought. He could finish his drinking from the bottle he had in his room.

He wanted nothing more to do with this crowd.

He swept his hair back off his forehead, put his hat on, and got the hell out of there before he wound up doing something unprofessional.

Chapter 3

He locked the hotel room door—for whatever good that might do, which he suspected was mighty little—and stripped down to his balbriggans and socks. The socks he kept on to keep from getting other people's dirt on his feet. When he threw the covers back, he saw that the foot of the sheets was muddy.

There was no washbasin in the cheesy room, so he contented himself with a mouth-cleansing swallow of Tom Moore from his travelling bottle and let it go at that.

He buckled his gunbelt and draped it over the iron headboard, trying first this way and then that until he found an angle that placed the butt of the revolver where he could find it quickly in the night. He expected no trouble here; there was no reason for it that he knew of, but still . . .

Got to watch yourself tonight, old son, he told himself. *Can't go putting holes in some traveler's belly if they send in somebody to share this here fifty-cent room.*

29

He lighted a final cheroot and sat on the edge of the sagging bed for a while to smoke it. While he sat there he felt of his rib cage. Nothing seemed to have been broken, but he was still sore. Likely would be for the next day or two.

He finished the cigar and flipped the butt out the open window, wishing a breeze would come up to cool the room down some. Even this late in the evening the air felt warm, almost hot.

Longarm sighed and stretched out on top of the bed, kicking the thin blanket down to the foot and covering himself only with the sheet. And that only out of habit.

He was asleep within seconds after he closed his eyes.

Longarm's fingers were wrapped around the grips of his Colt and he was pulling the gun from its holster before he realized that he was awake.

Consciousness returned. He blinked and looked toward the door that was still being opened. Apparently the turning of the knob or the snapping of the latch had been enough to waken him.

He kept his hand on the Colt while he waited to see who or what the intrusion was.

There was no light burning in the hallway, but a dim lessening of the darkness filtered to it from somewhere nearby. It was enough for him to identify a short person with a key in one hand and a valise in the other. Silhouetted outline was all he could make out, and very little of that, but it was enough. He relaxed and let the Colt slide back into the leather. This was just his bed partner for the night coming to turn in.

Longarm was not in a mood to be neighborly at the moment. He had been enjoying that sleep and intended to return to it. So, instead of greeting the newcomer and possibly losing half a night's sleep in idle conversation, he pressed his cheek back against the flimsy pillow the hotel provided and pretended he was still sleeping. He knew there was not enough light in the dark room for his bedmate to have seen his hand move.

He lay feigning sleep and listened drowsily while the other person relocked the hall door and bumped his way around the room in search of the furnishings.

Longarm knew when the newcomer found the bed. He walked smack into it, probably with a knee, and stifled a grunt of pain.

A questing hand touched Longarm's foot, but he did not move. The newcomer was determining which side of the bed to crawl into.

The sounds shifted to that side of the bed, and soon there was the faint thud of the valise being put down, then a soft rustling of cloth as the bedmate prepared to sleep.

Longarm wondered if he should warn the fellow about the state of the sheets, then decided that would be unwise. It would only lead to talk, and he really preferred sleep.

There was silence for a while, then the bed rocked and shifted as the other person sat gingerly on its edge. Whoever it was, Longarm thought, was being polite and quiet about joining him. He was grateful for that. Things could have been a whole lot worse.

The newcomer lay down with a low, weary sigh.

My sentiments exactly, Longarm thought.

For a time he fought against the pull of gravity as

the sagging mattress tried to roll him into the middle of the bed. But gradually he relaxed and let go. He slid comfortably back into the depths of a sound sleep.

Longarm woke to an acute sense of embarrassment. And a powerful hard-on.

While he had been sleeping, both he and his bed-mate had rolled and wiggled down into the deep hollow in the center of the bed. Now they were pressed together, back to belly, like a pair of spoons.

Longarm's crotch was tight and warm against his bedmate's rump. It was this contact, apparently, that had aroused his physical responses and brought him erect in his sleep.

Good grief, Longarm thought.

Cheeks burning, he tried to pull quietly away without waking the stranger who was sharing his hotel bed.

The problem was complicated by the fact that, probably as a natural part and parcel of the contact and the erection, he had also thrown an arm across the sleeping stranger's body, so now they were virtually locked together.

Longarm took the weight of his arm off the stranger and pulled back.

The palm of his hand encountered . . . a breast.

A breast?

It was unmistakable. Soft, yielding, mounded, feminine.

There could be no doubt about it.

Longarm's breath caught in his throat. He was still embarrassed, but considerably less so than he had been.

But what in hell was a strange woman doing in

this bed? Surely there was no hotel on earth that would deliberately expect a woman to share bed space with a man who was not her husband.

This was absolutely, utterly impossible. Longarm knew that. Yet that brief touch against the palm of his hand swore that it was so. And so, apparently, had his normal male instincts when he found his crotch pressed against her rump in the night.

Carefully, trying hard not to wake her, he withdrew his hand and arm. His fingertips trailed lightly over the swell of her hip. The touch was an accident. It was also a confirmation of what he already knew. Whoever this woman was, she was most definitely female in shape and substance. Her figure had a narrowness of waist and fullness of hip that no male would ever know.

She stirred slightly at his touch, although her breathing remained slow and deep. She was asleep but close to wakefulness.

Longarm's hard-on had sagged considerably from the shock of discovery. Now, as she moved and wriggled slightly in her shallow sleep, it intensified again, pressing against her with an unwanted insistence.

He tried to pull back away from her without disturbing her slumber, but now the slow cadence of her breathing changed as she shifted closer to waking. She mumbled something and pushed back against him to reestablish the contact.

Longarm held himself rigidly still, willing her to go back to sleep so he could get out of the bed and dress himself decently before . . .

She muttered something that might have been, "Yes, dear," and pushed herself backward again.

Mortified, Longarm lay still. She was as good as

awake now. Once she realized what was happening she was sure to scream. And even deputy marshals were not immune from charges of rape.

Her lips fluttered softly with an exhalation, and Longarm breathed more easily himself. She was going back to sleep, he thought.

Then, damn it, she sighed, and this time said clearly and lucidly, "Just a min, hon."

He could feel her hand moving on the far side of her body, could feel the faint, sliding tug against the sheet that covered them both.

She reached down along her thigh to find the hem of her nightdress, or whatever undergarment she was wearing as a substitute, and draw it up to her waist.

He could feel the difference immediately. Her bare flesh was warm through the thin cotton fabric of his balbriggans. Her skin was steamy hot now against him where the front of his thighs pressed against the backs of hers.

And he was uncomfortably aware that his erection had brought his cock creeping out between the buttons that closed the fly of his balbriggans. The long, rigid weight of him was nestled against the deep, warm vee between the cheeks of her rather ample ass.

He tried to pull away, still concerned about rousing her to full consciousness of this strange situation, but she reached behind her to find and guide him, leading him forward and arching her back, positioning him at the damp, furry entrance, guiding and drawing him.

She was still balanced on the thin edge that lay between sleep and awareness.

She pushed herself backward, enveloping him with hot flesh, silently taking the head of his penis into herself.

34

Longarm gritted his teeth and tried to resist his impulses.

She shoved backward again, impaling him deeper as they lay side by side, back to belly.

Slowly, almost inperceptibly at first, but then with a growing insistence, she began to pump her hips back and forth while Longarm lay still partially within her.

He moaned quietly to himself, and silently noted that the woman's breathing had steadied. She was almost fully asleep again, reacting obviously from habit, her senses too dulled by sleep for her to realize that she was in a strange bed now, with a man she did not know.

Longarm found himself responding to her small movements with answering movements of his own, his pelvis gently and slowly rocking backward and forward with a will of its own.

Sleepily she found his hand and brought it up to rest at her waist while she continued slowly to accommodate his male needs.

Longarm moaned slightly. He tried to resist for another few moments, but he was already inside her. His body and hers were already betraying them both. The wet, slippery contact had already gone too far.

He lay where he was and slowly, gradually extended the length of his thrusts, sliding deeper into her with each succeeding stroke until all of him was within her.

He heard her then, a short, sighing intake of breath, and she wriggled back against him harder, pressing the warmth of her rump against his belly.

He continued to stroke, slowly still, but deliberately now. He could hear her breath quicken. She found his hand and squeezed it, then pulled his hand around until he was draped across her hips, his fingertips tangled in a soft, hairy bush.

He knew what she wanted. While he continued to stroke into her, while she pressed herself to him, his fingers found first the moisture and then the heat of her opening. He found the tiny button of her pleasure and lightly stroked it with the pad of his forefinger while he continued to fill her and withdraw, fill and withdraw.

Her movements came faster now and harder. Her hips bucked and shoved, quicker, stronger.

After a little while she stiffened. Her body went rigid, and she clamped her thighs tightly together as she arched her back.

She cried out, a short, soft sound in the night, then sighed.

When she was done she relaxed so completely it felt like she was melting under his touch.

He was still within her. Still stroking lightly in and out.

He thought her breathing was drifting once again toward the slow, deep patterns of sleep. She had never really wakened.

She was done, but he was not. And somehow the total vulnerability of her responses was building him to a climax he had not really intended.

He felt the rising pressure deep in his groin, the tightening of unseen muscles, the gathering of super-heated, demanding fluids somewhere within him, the slight contraction of his balls.

He clamped an iron control of effort and will on his responses, determined that he would not thrash or grab at the final moment. He would not wake her.

The pressure continued to rise. When he came it

was in a long, slow flood, a quiet outpouring of intense pleasure that flowed from his body deep into hers.

Longarm was silent, but she sighed once more and moved herself against him in an instinctive response to the acceptance of his seed.

Longarm was drained, exhausted and sweaty, when finally he withdrew from her and rolled onto his back.

He had to hook an elbow over the side of the bed before he could pull himself away from the woman, out of the sagging depression in the middle of the bed, and finally swing his feet over until he was perched on the edge of the bed.

He felt weak and curiously shaky, so great had been the depth of the slow, intense release.

He rose as quietly as he could, found his things, and dressed. He did not want the embarrassment or the problems of what might happen when this woman, whoever she was and whatever she looked like, woke in the morning and remembered.

Cheeks burning at the very thought of it, Longarm got the hell out of there.

As he tiptoed to the door in stockinged feet and pulled it lightly closed, he stopped in the hall to pull his boots on and gather his gear together.

He glanced up at the door, then dug the room key out of his pocket and looked at the number on the tag.

Nine. The bat at the desk had given him room number nine.

Now the metal curlicue that identified the room numbers showed that this was number six.

He was puzzled for a moment. Then he looked closer and saw that the number had been affixed to the door with a single wire nail. A twist of the device could convert the nine to a six or back again.

An accident? Longarm walked quietly down the hall to examine the door that had said six when he came in last night. Now that one, also applied with a single nail, showed it was room nine.

Longarm grinned. He remembered the mischievous brats he had seen when he checked in. Fun and games time. He felt almost grateful to the little monsters now.

He pulled his watch from his vest pocket. Five o'clock. He could spend the rest of the dark hours in the hotel lobby.

And actually, he thought, he felt rather good now. There was a pleasantly hollow sensation low in his belly.

But he did rather wonder who the woman had been, and what she would think in the morning.

He picked up his gear and carried it down to the lobby.

A lamp was burning there, and someone had discarded a day-old copy of the Denver *Post*. Longarm lighted a cheroot and settled in for the rest of the night with the newspaper open in his lap.

Chapter 4

There must have been an early train scheduled for departure in one direction or the other, because by six o'clock, just about the time the soon-to-rise sun was bringing a gray paleness to the windows, the lobby was full of travelling men coming down to check out of the hotel and find their way into the restaurant that occupied much of the ground floor.

The place was full of noise and sleepy-eyed argument as the men, most of whom looked like seedy salesmen, paid their bills or coughed on their first morning cigars.

Longarm's attention was drawn from the men toward another early riser coming down the short flight of stairs.

It was a woman, very prim and ladylike, with her dark auburn hair piled high in a carefully arranged style of curls and coils. She was of average height and had a figure that even a Mother Hubbard missionary dress could not have hidden. Her travel dress, a medium shade of silky green, made no attempt to conceal the small waist or the full swell of bosom.

She was pretty enough to turn heads and stop the flow of conversations throughout the lobby. She must have been accustomed to that, yet she paused on the staircase and blushed a bright, startling red. The color at her cheeks made her all the more attractive, Longarm thought.

She stood there for a moment, blushing, and quickly glanced from one man to another.

Longarm brought the newspaper up quickly to hide the smile that crept unbidden to his lips. He peered over the top of it, enjoying her confusion.

She looked at the paunchy, balding man who was at the hotel desk at the moment, at a floridly handsome drummer whose loud vulgarities robbed him of any hope for dignity, at a skinny, none-too-clean man wearing yellow spats and a brocade vest. She looked at each of the men in the room, then dropped her eyes toward her shoes and blushed all the more furiously.

That answers that, Longarm thought. *She remembers, all right.*

She looked like a virtuous woman. There was a wedding band on her ring finger. He hoped she would be able to convince herself that she had only had a dream in the night.

Hard to do, he thought, but with luck she could talk herself into it.

He honestly hoped she would not be harmed by the encounter, but there was nothing he could do now to change a bit of it.

He debated speaking with her, explaining. But that, he finally decided, would only make things worse. If he did that, there would be no way she could ever make herself believe that her stop in Wray had involved nothing more terrible than a fantasy.

She was awfully pretty, though. More so the more he looked at her. Deliberately he raised the open newspaper another few inches to hide himself from her.

The next time he looked, she was gone. Into the restaurant, he was sure.

He laid the newspaper aside, picked up his carpetbag and saddle, and left the hotel, turning toward the cafe where he had gotten such a good supper the night before.

He felt a twinge of regret as he walked. He would have liked to meet the woman. Circumstances prevented that from ever being possible.

Breakfast turned out to be as good as supper had been. As he paid, he asked the proprietor about the stage schedule north to Holyoke.

"No stages at all running out of here any more," the man said. "Everybody goes by the trains nowadays."

"Are you trying to tell me that you can't get there from here?" Longarm asked with a smile.

"No such thing," the man told him. "Feller can get most anywhere if he wants to bad enough. But you won't be doing it by no stagecoach in these modern times."

"Would you direct me to the livery, then?"

"That I could do, sir," the restaurant man said cheerfully. "Tell him I sent you. He'll give you a good deal on the rental."

"Thanks," Longarm said. He hoped, however, that he would have better fortune at the livery than he had found at the saloon this same gentleman had recommended.

He waited for directions to the livery—although

41

it would have been fairly difficult for anyone to get lost in a town the size of Wray—and carried his gear to the low, rambling barn and set of corrals on the outskirts of town.

No one seemed to be tending the place when Longarm got there. He set his bag and saddle down beside the wide sliding doors at the front of the barn and whistled.

Looking inside, he saw movement in one of the stalls. A moment later the hostler came into view. He was a chubby, pimple-faced youngster, probably still in his teens. The boy had a slow-witted look about him, and seemed to be embarrassed about something. Longarm wondered briefly what it was that he had been doing in the empty stall. Something he should not have, that was obvious. But whether he had been napping or pulling his pecker or rolling a forbidden cigarette, Longarm had no way to judge.

"Mornin'," the boy said.

"Good morning."

"You wanta hire somethin'?"

"A horse."

The boy paused to remember what he had been told, then recited it slowly. "Twenty cent a day, sir, if you use our tack or fifteen if you got your own, sir." He finished, stopped to review what he had said, and then grinned proudly when he realized he had recited all of it.

"I have my own saddle, so I guess it will be fifteen cents."

The boy thought for a moment, then smiled. "Yes, sir."

"I only need a mount one way. Up to Holyoke. Will it be all right if I leave the animal there?"

"Uh-oh." The youngster gave that some thought. Then he brightened. "If you want, sir, I got two horses here as belong up there. You could take both of 'um back." He dug in his pocket for a stub of pencil and began figuring with it in the palm of his hand, his pudgy face a study in deep concentration.

"What are you trying to figure, son?"

"One day to Holyoke, sir. Two horses. I . . ."

"Whoa," Longarm said. "I don't need but one horse. I don't intend to pay for two and only ride one."

"Oh." The boy looked confused.

"I tell you what," Longarm said. "I'll pay you for the use of one horse and lead the other one home for you, and I won't charge you anything for doing that. Would that be all right?"

The kid had to think about that for a minute, then he beamed and nodded. "I won't get in no trouble for that, sir."

"Do you get in trouble a lot, son?"

"Yes, sir." The boy looked and sounded very sad about that.

"Well, I think your boss will find you've come up with a good piece of business this time. I'm sure he will be pleased with you."

"You really think so? Gee." The boy hurried to get both of the visiting horses. He fed and watered them with genuine care, then insisted on saddling for Longarm.

The horses had been brought from Holyoke with saddles on them and Longarm had his own McClellan, so the third saddle was loaded on top of the saddle of the horse Longarm intended to lead.

"There you are, sir," the boy said with pride when he was finished.

43

Longarm tied his carpetbag behind the cantle of the McClellan. He expected no trouble along the way, but in case anything happened he did not want to be separated from his things.

Longarm paid the boy fifteen cents but did not bother to ask the kid for directions to Holyoke. He wanted to end up there, after all, and not in New Mexico, which was way the hell and gone in the opposite direction.

"Thanks, son. You've done real good."

"Thank *you,* sir." The boy acted genuinely pleased to have been complimented. He stood in front of the barn doors and waved happily as long as Longarm was in sight.

The country was hardly exciting to ride through, hardly spectacular. It was mile after mile of bunchgrass and soapweed, rarely anything taller or more interesting than a sprig of sagebrush.

The mountains were far out of sight to the west. Here the highest point in view would be the next inevitable rise that would have to be topped and crossed in order to reach the one beyond that to the north.

The land rolled, one gentle mound after another, stretching as far as a man could see, and probably for many miles beyond that as well.

As far as Longarm could tell there were no bluffs, no mesas, no abrupt, choppy features at all that might have given the terrain character.

There was only more and more of the same low swells, the same bunchgrass, the same soapweed.

Thrilling, Longarm thought as he reined the livery horse to a halt so he could ease his back with a good stretch and pause to light a cheroot.

Also hot.

He squinted against the glare of sun from a cloud-less sky and reached up to loosen his collar and pull his string tie down a few inches. He removed his coat, folded it, and tied it on top of the carpetbag that was riding behind his cantle.

He glanced at the sky. The sun was already drop-ping toward the distant horizon, and he had not yet come twenty miles from Wray.

It was something between thirty-five and forty miles to Holyoke, the man back in Wray had said. A single day's ride.

Longarm grunted to himself and chewed on the butt of his cigar. A single day, maybe, if a man was able to cover some ground. He glanced over his shoul-der with some distaste at the second, led horse. The idiot grulla was balky, nasty, and hard to get along with. That would have been just fine except that it was also a pain in the ass to lead. If it had not been for the second horse, he probably would have been within sight of his destination by now. As it was, he was still planted out here in the middle of nowhere with night only a few hours off and many miles yet to be covered.

Resigned to spending a night with the ground for his bed, Longarm bumped the bay horse he was riding into a walk, which was all he could manage with that damned grulla pulling back against the lead every foot of the way.

At least, he thought ruefully, the ground here was not as hard as it was further south. A few miles south the soil was baked clay, much like a caliche, and nearly as hard as granite. At least here the soil was loose, friable, and sandy. Things could have been worse, he thought as he finished the cheroot and tossed the butt away.

He bedded down at dusk. He carried only one pair of hobbles in his saddlebags. Those he put on the bay. For a moment he was tempted to let the damn grulla wander. If the bastard went away during the night, his trip would be all that much easier in the morning.

But, damn it, he was responsible for the beast. He fashioned a makeshift set of hobbles from the strings on one of the livery saddles, stripped the bridles from both horses, and turned them loose to graze. The bay he gave a rubdown; the grulla he did not.

There was no wood for a fire, so he made do with dried cow patties—although why there should be so much cow shit on the ground in a country where he was seeing no cattle was a puzzlement—and brewed a pot of coffee.

Supper was jerked beef and a few cold biscuits he had picked up at breakfast time. The menu had been the same for his lunch.

When he was finished eating, the coffee was stoutly boiled. He poured some into a tin cup, tasted it, and decided it needed strengthening. A healthy slug of Maryland rye whiskey and a two-fingered dip of sugar provided that. He stirred the brew with a grass stem, tasted again, and approved of the result.

"Better," he said aloud. He realized what he had done and looked around quickly to make sure there was no one near who could have heard him talking to himself. There was no one and nothing in sight except his own campfire and the two horses that were busy cropping the rich, sun-cured brown bunch-grasses.

The bay heard him. The horse lifted its muzzle to

look at him with its ears tilted in his direction. "Yeah," he lied, "I'm talking to you."

The bay blew, spraying snot from its fluttering nostrils, and went back to grazing.

"So much for conversation," Longarm said.

He finished the coffee and helped himself to another, this time without the sweetening and with much less coffee in the cup. He held the dark brown bottle up to the faint light from his cow-chip fire. It was more than half full. He took a snort from the bottleneck, replaced the cork, and went back to the coffee. The heat of it was satisfying in his belly, and the stars were startling in their clarity overhead. Longarm removed his vest and gunbelt and lay back against the seat of his McClellan, using it for a pillow. The night was too warm to require a blanket. He closed his eyes and let himself go.

Hoofbeats brought him into an abrupt sitting position with the Colt in his hand. He looked first for his own horses, thinking they might somehow have slipped their hobbles and be on their way home without him.

The moon was up, though, and he could see both horses standing not a hundred yards off with their heads raised and ears pricked. They were looking off toward the west, toward the sound of hard-drumming hoofs. A glance toward the circling stars showed Longarm that the night was only half gone.

A man on horseback topped a rise to the west, moving fast, and dipped out of sight again almost immediately. Moments later the dark figure reappeared in silhouette at the top of the nearest rise. The rider was leaning low over the horse's withers, urging it on.

47

The animal was tired, though. It was paddling with both forefeet, and its head and neck were surging up and down entirely too much. The gait was labored.

They swept nearer, stretching out on the downhill run, and Longarm could hear the ragged breathing.

"What the . . . ?"

The rider heard. He seemed not to have noticed Longarm until the deputy spoke. Now he gave Longarm a wide-eyed stare as he raced past the remains of Longarm's fire. It took a second or two for the unexpected presence to register. Then he sat upright and threw his weight back against the cantle as he hauled on his reins.

The jaded horse slid to a choppy, ungraceful stop and stood gratefully with its head low and legs trembling. The rider dropped out of his saddle and came running back to Longarm.

"Where's your horse, mister? I'll make you a trade." He sounded almost as breathless as his mount.

Longarm tilted his head to the side and listened. He could hear more hoofbeats now, sounds made by many more than one horse. They were moving just as fast as this man had been.

"You wouldn't have time," Longarm said, "even if I was agreeable to it. Which I ain't."

"You got no choice, mister," the man said, reaching toward a holstered revolver that rode high on his right hip. Whatever else this cowboy was—and Longarm could see now that he was little more than a boy in a big hat—he was no gunman. He had not even noticed the dark steel of the big Colt in Longarm's hand.

"Wrong," Longarm said. He thumbed back the hammer of the Thunderer. The double-action mechanism made that unnecessary for firing, but the oiled

48

cla-clack provided a telltale sound that was unmistakable.

"Oh," the cowboy said.

"Uh-huh."

"Mister, I got to—"

"Huh-uh. You don't 'got to' and you ain't going to." For the sake of his own safety, although he had no idea yet what was going on here, Longarm stepped forward and relieved the boy of the revolver he had been carrying. It was a Smith & Wesson Schofield, rugged and accurate, but woefully clumsy and slow. No, the kid was no gunhand. Longarm tucked the Smith into the waist of his trousers and waited.

The boy's pursuers thundered over the last rise, five or six of them, and raced down toward the camp.

"Those horses are fresher," Longarm observed in a soft voice. "You wouldn't have got away from them."

The riders came to a dust-boiling halt with rifles and revolvers waving in every direction. They were all shouting at once. There were seven of them, Longarm saw now that he could make a count at close range.

One of them, a thick-bodied man with enough gray in his beard that it was visible even by moonlight, spurred his horse closer and leveled a revolver at the boy standing at Longarm's side.

"You do and I'll drop you sure as shit," Longarm said calmly. There was fine-honed steel in his voice, though, and his intentions could not have been in doubt.

The man with the pistol looked at Longarm for the first time. "Stand aside, man. This isn't your affair."

"You could be right, but until I decide that I'll finish any shooting you care to start."

"Stand aside, man." The man waved his revolver from side to side, trying to peer around Longarm. The boy, wisely enough, had sidled around to put Longarm between himself and the men with the guns.

"I'm Deputy United States Marshal Custis Long, riding out of the Denver marshal's office," Longarm said loud enough for all to hear. "And who might you be, sir?"

The rider looked startled. Behind him some of his men began to lower their weapons.

"You sure about that?" the rider asked.

"Yeah, I don't have a lick of trouble remembering who I am. Now what about you?"

The man was still angry and stirred up, but he was beginning to calm a little now. "I s'pose you got identification on you?"

"Yes, but I don't intend to turn my back while you boys are waving all that iron."

The man grunted, then let down the hammer on his single-action Colt and shoved the revolver into his holster. "Put 'em away, boys. I reckon a legal hanging's as good as a bellyful of lead for the little son of a bitch." The other riders followed their leader's example.

Their boss dismounted and then so did the rest of them. "Build up that fahr, Grunt. Get some light on the subject," the leader ordered. One of the riders grunted an acknowledgement of the order and began to pile dried cow chips on the coals from Longarm's fire.

"Kind of free with another man's camp, aren't you," Longarm said.

"My range," the man said. "I'll be free with it if I damn well please. Now show me them credentials."

Standing face to face as they now were, Longarm could see that the man, who had still not identified himself, was a head shorter than Longarm but wider in the body and shoulders. He looked like he might have been a real bull of the woods not too many years ago, and he acted like he thought he still was.

Longarm untied his coat from the McClellan and found his wallet. He opened it and struck a match so the cowman could see it, but did not hand the wallet to the man. "Your turn," he said.

"I'm Nate Maberly," he announced. His voice held considerable pride, as if the name was supposed to mean something.

"So?"

"I said—"

"Oh, I heard that part. But where's the rest, Maberly? Where's your badge? Your warrant? You do have such, don't you?"

The fire flared up in time for Longarm to see Maberly's face color and his jaw take on a grim set of anger.

"Uh-huh," Longarm said. "Your badge and your warrant are .45 caliber. Am I right?"

"Now you listen to me, Lang. You step aside an' let me have that stinking little cow thief, or I'll have your badge to hang on my wall."

"And a right fine wall I'm sure it is, Maberly," Longarm said. "And I'll be right glad to give you my name again, which happens to be Long, Custis Long, and the U.S. marshal's name an' address. If you figure you can have my badge for a decoration, well, you're free to go for it. Meantime, though, I'll be considering whether I should put the cuffs on you for attempted murder and interference with an officer. Or would you

51

rather tell me what it is this boy is supposed to have done?"

Maberly blustered and cursed for a minute, until Longarm palmed his Colt and pulled out a set of handcuffs.

"I didn't say..."

"That's right," Longarm agreed. "You didn't say. Which is the point I been trying to make. So why don't you tell me what it is that's disturbing my sleep."

Maberly growled and grumped some more. Finally he came to the point. "It's him," he said, pointing past Longarm's shoulder toward the kid who was taking refuge at Longarm's back. Maberly acted like that explained everything.

Longarm sighed. "This may amaze you, Nate, but I'd kind of suspected that all along."

"He's a damned rustler, Long. We caught the little son of a bitch red-handed. And I do mean red. Still had the blood on his hands and a quarter of meat tied on his saddle. That's a hanging offense, damn it, and I expect to see him hung."

"That's right, Deputy. We caught him sure this time," one of Maberly's men added. "Me and Johnny seen him. We went an' got the rest of the crowd. He run when he seen us coming."

Longarm turned to the kid behind him. "Well?"

The boy looked frightened. In the better light of the fire he looked younger than Longarm had first thought, sixteen, perhaps even less than that. He said nothing, his eyes locked on Nate Maberly's hatred.

Longarm touched his arm. "What's your name, boy?"

The kid swallowed. "Wright, sir. Tim Wright."

"All right, Tim. What's your side of it?"

The boy swallowed again and seemed unable to speak. Without warning he blushed and turned his back, making a futile, fluttering gesture with his right hand. Longarm's lips tightened in a thin smile of understanding. If he was reading that hand movement correctly, Tim had been so scared he wet himself and did not want anyone to see.

Longarm turned back to Maberly's riders. "You," he said, pointing. "Do me the favor of fetching his horse over here to the fire, would you?"

"Yes, sir, Marshal."

Wright's tired animal was standing not fifty yards away, but the cowhand mounted his own horse to go and lead it in rather than walk fifty yards.

Longarm accepted the reins from him. "Yep," he said, "there's a quarter of fresh meat tied on here. You." He pointed toward the hand who had spoken to back Maberly a moment ago. "Tell me exactly what you saw before you went to get the rest of the boys."

"You bet," the man said. "I seen this kid lift that there meat up an' tie it behint his saddle. He seen me about the same time, I think, 'cause he was gonna bend down an' get some more, but he never. 'Stead, he got up on his horse an' headed for home."

"Pretty small haunch," Longarm said.

"Musta been a calf," the cowhand said.

"You saw the calf, did you?"

"Not exactly. Didn't have to."

"You could see Tim, but you couldn't see the dead calf?"

"That's right," the rider declared. "'Twas down in a swale, like. I couldn't see the kid's horse but from the hocks up neither, but I seen enough to know it was a horse. An' I seen that haunch he was tyin', which is right there 'fore your own eyes now."

Longarm nodded. "Thanks." He looked at Maberly. "And I take it now you'd like to swear out a complaint against Tim for killing one of your calves?"

"Damn right I would. Though it would have been easier for everybody if you'd left us alone to do what had to be done."

"You'd have killed a boy over a two-dollar calf, is that it, Maberly?"

"It isn't the money, damn it. It's the principle of the thing. I didn't get where I am by letting a bunch of damn nesters steal my cows, you can believe that."

"Oh, I believe that, all right," Longarm said. "Is that what's really graveling you, Maberly? That some folks have come in here trying to make a living on land that belongs to them as much as it does to you? Is that it?"

"You said that, Long. Not me."

"Uh-huh. So I did." Longarm turned to Tim. "Is there anything you want to tell them, boy?"

Tim still would not turn to face them where the crotch of his jeans might have been seen in the firelight. "They wouldn't believe me nohow, Marshal, sir."

"Probably not, son, but they might believe themselves." He turned back to Maberly's crowd. "You. Grunt, is it? Would you kindly untie that haunch and drop it here by the fire so we can all get a look at it?"

Grunt shrugged and went to Tim's horse. He began to untie the fresh, bloody haunch, then stopped. He looked back at Longarm.

"That's right," Longarm said. "That's the only meat I see tied there. Bring it over so we can all get a look at it."

54

"What the hell are you up to, Long?" Maberly demanded.

Longarm folded his arms and did not bother to answer. The rider called Grunt was red-faced, and it could not have been from exertion, as he carried the small haunch over into the firelight and deposited it on the ground.

"Aw, shit," one of the Maberly men said. He began to look sick as he turned away from the fire. He mounted his horse and rode away without waiting for the others. Probably, Longarm thought, the man who was leaving now was the best of the lot of them.

Longarm glared at them, and their eyes would not meet his. Heads turned. And then the men turned. Slowly, one by one, they mounted and left, until only Maberly was standing there.

The aging cowman did not look a lick repentant. His continuing hard-assed attitude pissed Longarm off.

"Aren't you going to say anything, Maberly?"

"Nothing to say," the man declared. "The little son of a bitch is still a thief."

Rage boiling in him now, Longarm's hand lanced out to tangle in Maberly's beard. He jerked the man's head around and pulled him down to his knees directly above the haunch of fresh meat.

"Look at it, damn you. Look at it. Does that look like any damn calf to you?"

Maberly stared unblinking toward the antelope haunch, its distinctive tan, white, and black hide coloration plain on the unskinned hindquarter.

"This time—" Maberly began.

Longarm snatched him upright, still hanging onto the old bastard's beard. He leaned down until he was

55

nose to nose with Maberly and snarled, "This time, mister, is the last time. You understand me?"

"I understand."

"Shut up, you miserable old asshole. Listen to me when I'm talking. This time you would have killed a boy over a piece of wild meat. If there's a next time, by God, I'll hear about it. I'll be putting a flyer out, Maberly. It will be going to every peace office, state and local and federal, that has anything to do with this country *and* to the Cattlemen's Association *and* to every justice of the peace in northeast Colorado and southwest Nebraska *and* to anybody else I can think of when I ain't so damn hot and can think clearer. But you better know it, Maberly. I'm putting the word out. Anything happens to this boy or any of his kin, even anything *legal* happens to them, and I'm gonna be on you like stink on shit. You understand that, Maberly? Do you?"

He took a wrap on Maberly's beard and twisted hard, and the older man cried out and fell to his knees when Longarm released him.

"Do you understand me?"

"Yes," Maberly hissed.

"Then get out of my sight before I lose my temper, you old shit."

Maberly stood. He stood for a moment facing Longarm, his legs braced wide. Longarm could see in the man's eyes that he was thinking about it.

"Go ahead," Longarm said. "The pleasure would be mine."

Maberly's resolve disappeared. His shoulders slumped. "If I was younger..."

"If you was younger you wouldn't be able to walk before I let you leave this camp. Now *git!*"

Maberly got.

Longarm watched him out of sight, then turned back to Tim Wright. "Better unsaddle that horse, son, and give it a good rubdown."

"My ma will be worried, sir. I better get home to her."

"Then rub the horse down and give it a little rest first. It won't be carrying you anywhere for a few days. I have a spare animal over there you can ride, and I'll go with you. I can head on to Holyoke from there, wherever your place is, come daybreak."

"Yes, sir." The boy hesitated. "Mister Marshal, sir . . ."

"It's all right, Tim. I understand."

The boy bobbed his head. "Thank you, sir." He went to do as Longarm said.

Chapter 5

Even going as slowly as they had to in order to accommodate Tim Wright's exhausted horse, they reached the Wright homestead in little more than an hour. It was late by then, just short of two o'clock in the morning by Longarm's dependable Ingersol, but there was a candle burning in the window.

"I told you she'd be worried," Tim said when he saw the light. "What d'you want to bet she's waiting up for me in that old rocking chair of hers?"

"What about your pa, Tim?"

"He's dead, Marshal. Killed better than a year ago, it was."

Longarm's eyes flashed. "Nate Maberly, boy?"

"Sir? Oh." Tim shook his head. "Nothing like that, Marshal. A horse went down with him. He hit his head on a rock, an' he was gone. Me and Ma and the little kids been trying to make out since, but it ain't easy. That's why . . . well, why we need that meat so bad. We don't own a rifle, just Pa's old scattergun, and that don't have the range for shooting antelope, which is about all the game we have around here. I was lucky to've got one with the pistol." He shook his head. "Sure wished I'd've had time to get the rest of the critter loaded, but when I seen that man I knew I'd better skeedaddle."

"You did the right thing, Tim. Maybe in the morning we can spot a few of those loud-colored prairie goats, and I can knock some down for you. Do you know how to jerk meat?"

"Yes, sir, I can handle that."

"All right. If you can put me into a bunch of them, I'll shoot all I can bring down. That will give you some meat to get you through the winter."

"I'd appreciate it, Marshal. We all of us would."

"No problem," Longarm assured him. "One favor, though."

"Just you name it, sir."

"My friends call me Longarm. That would sound better to me than all this 'sir' stuff."

The boy grinned. "I'd be real proud to have you for a friend." The grin got wider. "Longarm."

Longarm nodded and smiled at him.

The door of the cabin, which turned out to be a low soddy dug halfway into the slope of one of the many rises, burst open a good fifty yards before they reached it.

Candlelight spilled out onto the packed earth in front of the place, and a woman's figure rushed out into the yard. Longarm could not see her features with the light behind her, but he could see that she was slender, not especially tall, and that her hair was hanging loose.

She was nicely built for a woman old enough to have a nearly grown son, he thought as the candlelight behind her outlined her body against the thin cotton of her nightdress. It was rather apparent that she had not been expecting a visitor to be with her son.

Tim jumped down from the grulla he was riding, and his mother ran to him. She wrapped her arms around him and began to cry.

The boy soothed her. At the same time he looked over his shoulder toward Longarm with a half embarrassed, half apologetic expression. He need not have worried. Longarm understood.

"Ma," he said when he could finally get a word in edgewise. "I'd like you to meet a . . . a friend of mine. He's a Newnited States deputy marshal, an' he said I can call him Longarm like his other friends do." He was grinning proudly.

Mrs. Wright looked worried again. "Is there . . . has there been any trouble?"

"Mind if I step down, ma'am? We'll tell you all about it."

"Of course not, I . . . *oh!*" She glanced down at her state of undress and clamped a horrified hand over her mouth. Before Longarm or Tim could say anything more, she turned and raced back inside the soddy.

Longarm laughed and reached for a cheroot. "Let's give your ma a minute to get herself together, son. Then we'll do the tellin'."

Later, with Mrs. Wright swaddled in a quilted robe that must have been uncomfortably warm, Longarm sat at their table while the woman served him a cup of sage tea. She apologized for not being able to offer him coffee.

"This will be just fine, ma'am." He took a sip of the range-picked brew and was able somehow to refrain from making a face at the bitter taste. Thank

61

goodness it had not been steeped any longer or stronger.

"Tell your ma what happened, Tim. I want to fetch something from my saddlebags."

"Bring your things inside, Marshal. Please. We certainly owe you some hospitality," Mrs. Wright said.

"You don't owe me a thing, ma'am, and I wouldn't think of imposing. If it's all right, though, I'll bed down in your shed for the rest of the night."

She acted like she wanted to protest, perhaps to offer her own bed and she would sleep with the children, but Tim was excitedly telling her about his narrow escape from Maberly.

Longarm went out and got his food sack from his saddlebags. There was not much in there, not nearly as much as he would have liked, but there was still plenty of the sugar he had been carrying. He suspected it had been some time since any of the Wrights had had real sugar to taste.

While he was outside he unsaddled all three horses and turned them loose in the small pen Wright had built downwind of the soddy. He dumped his gear and the saddles under the overhang of a dugout shed and carried the food sack inside. By the time he returned, Tim had finished his tale.

Mrs. Wright gave Longarm a wide-eyed look of gratitude and impulsively took his hand. "There is no way we could ever thank you enough, Marshal."

"I told you, ma'am, no thanks are necessary. It was just a matter of being able to help, and glad that I could too." He put the sack on the table and opened it. "Here, ma'am. I thought you might enjoy a little sweetenin' for your tea."

"Oh, I couldn't, Marshal, but you go right ahead."

"Truth is," Longarm said, resuming his chair, "I

like it just fine the way it is." He proved it by taking a deep swallow of the vile brew. He finished the tea and smiled.

"Could I offer you something to eat, Marshal? I could fry you some mush. Or I could warm you some of the stew we had left from supper. I was saving it for Timmy. Wild onion and turnips, mostly."

Tim made a face, although Longarm could not guess whether it was from the thought of the root stew or because his mother had called him by such an un-grown-up name. It could have been either or both, Longarm thought.

"I'm not a bit hungry, ma'am. But I thank you."

Longarm looked toward the back of the soddy. There were several small, silent heads in evidence in the shadows back there. Three . . . no, four of them. The younger Wrights, obviously. He winked toward them and the smallest of the lot, who might have been either a boy or a girl, giggled.

Mrs. Wright smiled and blew out one of the candles she had had on the windowsill. She brought the other to the table. In its light Longarm could see that she had once been an unusually pretty woman, although now much of her beauty had faded under the pressures of hard work and poor food. She was still fairly at-tractive, but in a few more years she would be about as pretty as a cast-off shoe. He wondered about her age. She might have been anything from thirty to forty-five.

"If you would excuse me, ma'am, I'll go out and make up my bed. It's been a long day, and Tim and I want to get an early start tomorrow."

"You're going somewhere, Timmy?"

Tim proudly explained that he and his friend Long-

63

arm would be going hunting in the morning.

The boy looked confused when his mother burst into tears and ran into a back corner of the soddy. "Ma?"

"It's all right, Tim," Longarm said. He rose and squeezed the youngster's shoulder. "I understand, and it's all right. I'll see you at first light."

"Yes, sir."

Tim still looked confused, but he did not object when Longarm left to bed down in the shelter of the dugout shed.

"Marshal?" Her voice was a whisper in the night.

"I'm awake, ma'am." Longarm drew deeply on his final before-bed cheroot, faintly illuminating his face with a red glow. He was sitting in a corner of the shed with his blankets and saddle laid out nearby.

Mrs. Wright entered the dark shed slowly, feeling her way along the sod wall, and joined him. "I couldn't go to sleep without thanking you, Marshal."

"Longarm," he corrected.

"All right, Longarm. My . . . my name is Melba."

"Care to sit down, ma'am? I mean, Melba? There's a saddle on the floor there. Yeah, that's it."

She lost her balance for an instant as she tried to find the offered seat in the darkness. He caught and steadied her. For a moment her breath was warm against his cheek; then she withdrew and sat primly with her hands folded in her lap. "Was that . . . whiskey I smelled?"

"Yes, ma'am," he admitted. "If I've offended you by bringing liquor to your home . . ."

"No," she said quickly. "You don't offend me at all." She sighed. "When Jake was alive, he used to share a drink with me now and then. I rather enjoyed the warmth of it, you know, down in your stomach." She sighed again. "There hasn't been much warmth in my life since Jake died. Or in Timmy's. I really do appreciate your being so kind to him."

Longarm shrugged. "I like him. He seems like a nice kid."

"He is."

"Would you enjoy a drink, ma'am? I mean, Melba? I don't have any glasses, but . . ."

"Yes, I would." She accepted the bottle from him and took a small sip from the neck, then another.

Longarm's cheroot had gone out. He struck another match to relight it. In the flare of the match head he could see fresh tear tracks on her cheeks.

"It must be hard on you," he said.

The sympathetic words were enough to send her into a flow of fresh tears and open sobbing. She leaned toward him, and Longarm instinctively responded by putting his arms around her, trying to comfort her.

The hollow of his throat was moist with her tears, and she pressed herself closer against him. Her nearness aroused him, and he shifted his thigh to try to keep her from feeling the erection.

The motion came too late, though. She was already aware of it. Her breath caught in her throat and her tears quit flowing. She lay against his chest, poised halfway between flight and acquiescence.

He could feel her indecision in the tensions of her slim body. Then, with a sob that had nothing to do with tears, she pressed herself against him.

She raised her face, seeking his lips, and he obliged her with a kiss.

"So long," she murmured, her left hand stroking

his chest, opening buttons so she could slide her fingers onto the muscular, hairy planes of male skin there.

Longarm pulled her into his lap and slid down from the seat of the livery saddle onto the floor. She moved with him, eager for contact with his body, pressing herself tight against him.

He kissed her again and felt the quick, probing dart of her tongue into his mouth. He responded in kind.

"So long," she said again, and held him all the closer.

She turned slightly, offering herself openly, and his fingers fumbled with the buttons on the front of her nightdress.

The cloth parted and fell away. She was wearing no undergarments. Her breasts were full. The suckling of so many children had softened them; they sagged a little, but her nipples were firm and erect.

Longarm bent his head to her, drew one nipple into his mouth and then the other. He nipped at them with compressed lips, rolled them on his tongue. Melba Wright's head lolled weakly from side to side, and she moaned softly.

He gathered the hem of her cotton garment and pulled it higher. She parted her thighs, ready for his touch. He found the dark patch of soft hair. He probed with a finger and found the spot he wanted, and she began to moan louder, raising her hips to him. She was very wet, entirely ready.

Longarm kissed her again while he fingered her. Quickly, without warning, her hips began to pump and gyrate rapidly, and her breathing became ragged. Her eyes got wide, and a low, keening sound issued from her throat as she reached a sudden, short climax.

Longarm smiled and kissed her again.

Her movements were less insistent now. She found the buttons at his fly and undid them, then helped him out of his clothing.

He had to lie back to get his trousers and balbriggans off. When he did so she knelt over him, caressing him gently with both hands, running her fingers up and down the length of him, cupping his balls in her palms.

She bent over him. Her hair, long and loose in readiness for sleep, spilled down over his genitals. She pressed her cheek against him with a glad sigh, then nuzzled and licked at the base of his tool.

She shifted position, angling her hips toward his head, and lifted his balls with one hand while she used the other to support herself. Her head dipped lower, and her tongue flicked lightly over that intensely sensitive area. The tongue roved, darting, laving, up along his shaft to daintily circle the head of his member.

Longarm was completely aroused now. He reached for her and took her by the shoulders. He pulled her up until she was lying against him. They were separated only by a thin wrap of cotton wadded around her waist.

Her body felt soft and warm against his. Her arms slid around him, and she opened herself to him, tugging at him, urging him to mount her.

He knelt between her knees and lowered himself slowly. He found the entrance easily and slid a few inches into her waiting heat.

Melba gasped and pulled him deeper.

He pressed into her until his belly was against hers, until all of him was contained inside her. She accepted his weight and hugged him close, wrapping arms and legs around him and burying her face in his throat.

"So long," she said again, but this time he was not sure from her tone of voice if she was speaking about the passage of time or about him.

"Raise up," she whispered.

He did as she asked.

"Now hold still there. Can you do that?"

"Of course." He braced himself on his elbows, body rigid, while she lay impaled beneath him.

"Now let me," she asked.

Longarm held himself still as Melba began to raise her hips to him and then withdraw. With each stroke she pushed herself up onto him; with each withdrawal she sighed as if something had just been lost.

She set a slow, quiet pace for herself. She seemed to be enjoying every second of the deep, warm contact.

Gradually she moved faster and then faster yet. She began to pump vigorously, and her breath became ragged and quick again.

He could feel her spill over the edge of satiation. He could feel the tightening of her arms, the press of her slim thighs against his hips, the soft, convulsive clutch of her sex as it enveloped him.

She yelped softly and hung onto him with all her strength, with all of her body. Then she went limp.

Longarm, smiling and still firmly erect, relaxed and let his weight down onto her. Into her.

Melba's eyes went wide. "You haven't yet?"

"In a minute," he said gently. "There's no hurry." He smiled and kissed her. Her lips were soft, and her answering kiss had a gentle, dreamy quality to it.

After a little while he began to move within her. Very slowly at first, very shallowly, then with longer strokes and faster. He drew her along with him, pacing his movements to the rhythms that were being returned by her body.

When finally he tightened and jetted his seed deep inside her she was ready with him once more, and she spiralled over the same precipice of pleasure when he did.

He lay inside her, softer now, for a long time. When he tried to roll away and relieve her of his weight, she held onto him in protest.

"Please?" she asked.

"Of course."

It was late before she left the shed for the solitude of her widow's bed. Longarm did not regret the loss of sleep at all.

Chapter 6

"Just the other side of this rise, Longarm," Tim said in an excited whisper. "I don't know what it is they like there, salt or just a favorite place, but I see them there a lot."

Longarm nodded and pulled his Winchester from the scabbard, made sure he had some loose rounds of .44-40 in his coat pocket even though he knew there would be no possibility of having time to reload. As far as he knew, there was nothing in the world as fast as a frightened antelope.

"Wait here," Longarm told Tim. "When I stop shooting, get out your skinning knife and bring the horses over."

"Yes, sir," Tim said with a grin.

Longarm walked up the shallow slope. As he neared the top he crouched lower, then went to his knees and finally to his belly for the last few yards. He removed his hat and wriggled slowly ahead until he could see into the swale below.

As Tim had predicted, there were antelope there. Eighteen, perhaps twenty of them in the band. He did not take time to count.

The closest of them was not more than sixty yards away. The rest were strung out to a distance of a hundred and fifty yards or so.

The muzzle of the Winchester snaked forward, and Longarm took his time about sighting on the fattest, farthest animal he could see. The first shot would be the only one he could take his time with, and he wanted to make that one good.

He chose a plump doe for the sure kill. There was a buck slightly nearer with an impressive set of horns, but he was hunting meat, not horn. Horn would do damn little to feed a bunch of small children. The doe looked bigger, and its meat would be more tender.

He thumbed the hammer back, and the nearest of the herd, a small buck, probably a yearling, flicked its ears and swung its head to look. It could see him. Longarm knew that. But the young animal seemed not to know it should be frightened. It snorted and took a tentative step toward him.

Longarm placed the tip of the front sight immediately behind the point of his target's shoulder and squeezed.

The Winchester fired with a burst of artificial thunder, and the distant doe collapsed. The rest of the band added the thunder of their frantic hoofs to the echo of the rifle shot, and Longarm worked the lever of the Winchester with fluid, practiced speed.

Another antelope—buck or doe, he did not bother to look—obliged him by racing past the sights of the rifle. He held well in front of the running antelope even though the shot was a quartering one. He fired again, and the animal went down.

He worked the lever rapidly and snapped a shot at the last and the slowest of the herd. He had not led it quite enough. The distance was greater now, and the speed of the creatures was awesome. The antelope, another doe, fell with a slug in its left rear hip, then struggled up again on three legs.

He had slowed it. That was something. He came to his knees and put a finishing shot behind its shoulder.

Three down out of nearly two dozen antelope. That was all he had had time for. He thought about Melba Wright and her children and wished it could have been more.

He turned and scrambled down the slope to where he had left his hat. Being out of doors bareheaded after so many years of wearing a hat made him feel vaguely uneasy. There was no logical reason for that—it was habit, nothing else—but he felt it just the same.

Tim was already leading both horses up to him. "Well?"

Longarm held up three fingers, and the boy whooped with glee.

There would be steaks and roasts and stews in the Wright soddy for at least a little while, Longarm thought.

He accepted the reins of the grulla and the bay from Tim. "You can handle them now, can't you, son?"

"Yes, sir, I sure can."

"Then we'd best shake hands goodbye, Tim."

"But, Longarm . . ." The boy looked genuinely disappointed.

Longarm was sure the disappointment had nothing to do with being left with the chore of gutting and skinning three animals.

"I have work to do, Tim. It wouldn't be right for

me to stay here just because I want to and maybe let some poor folks be robbed because of my laziness. I got to get to it."

"Yes, sir." The boy dismounted and offered Longarm his hand. He acted like he would really have liked to give the tall deputy a hug. But that would have been unmanly, and Tim was the man of the place now. Hugs were for children. But his eyes were unnaturally bright at the thought of his new friend leaving.

"I'll come back this way if I can, son," Longarm promised.

Longarm mounted the grulla that was now wearing his old McClellan. Last night had proven that the grulla was a decent saddle horse even if it did lead with all the grace and will of a pine log. The bay, he had found as he and Tim rode out earlier in the morning, led the way a horse should. He likely could already have been in Holyoke and on the job if he had chosen to saddle the grulla back in Wray.

He looked at Tim, though, and was just as happy he had made the mistake. If he had gotten to Holyoke last night, things would have been bad for the Wright family this morning.

"Take care, Tim. I'll see you again." He touched a finger to the brim of his Stetson and turned the grulla north toward Holyoke.

The morning's ride was easy and the directions unmistakable. Holyoke was on the banks of Frenchman Creek.

"If you cross water an' keep going you've passed it," he had been told. "If you find the crick and don't see the town, toss a coin an' turn one way or th' other. If you ride alongside the crick and come to a bare, open trail, that's the Ogallala an' you got to turn around and go back west. If you run outa crick, that means you got to turn around and ride back east to the town. But you can't miss it."

As it turned out, it was even easier than that. About mid-morning he found a wagon road that led from some ranch straight to the town. He was there in time for lunch.

He turned the horses and their saddles in at the Holyoke livery and walked out into the street to get a look at the community.

There was not all that much to see. Even less than down in Wray, where they had the railroad to encourage commerce.

Holyoke consisted of fewer than two dozen homes, a school that apparently did double duty as the church judging from the cross erected above the traditional bell cupola, a handful of stores, a smithy, and one saloon. There was no bank and no government offices. If Holyoke had its own peace officer, he was keeping himself hidden.

Which, Longarm thought without displeasure, eliminated any necessity to pay a courtesy call on the local law. He wanted to be able to take a look at the stage line's problems without that, if he could. It looked like he could.

He picked up his gear and walked into the center of the business district, which from the livery stable was a distance of not more than two hundred yards.

The street and the few stores did not seem very busy at this time of day. The busy time in this cow country, Longarm knew, would be early evening and on Saturdays. The rest of the week everyone would be working.

There was no stage station in the town, but a sign

nailed over the door of a general mercantile store said Simmons Express Company. That was the crowd he wanted.

He stepped inside the store and was grateful for the cooling relief of the shade indoors. It was hot as hell out there in the sun.

There were no customers in the store at the moment. The clerk, probably also the proprietor in a place this size, was perched on a tall stool with a newspaper spread open on the bare counter before him. He looked up when Longarm came in, removed his reading glasses, and laid them on the newspaper. "What can I do for you today, mister?"

Longarm set his saddle and bag down beside the door and approached the counter. "I need some information about the next stage to Julesburg," he said.

The man nodded. "Schedule's always the same," he said. "Comes down one day, goes back the next. Today it's due to come down. Tomorra morning it leaves to go back. Same every day except Sunday. They don't run on Sundays."

"Should I buy my ticket now and avoid the rush?"

The storekeeper laughed. "Tell you what, friend. If it comes to that, I'll personally throw a little old lady off the thing to make sure there's room for you. Is that fair?"

"I couldn't ask fairer," Longarm said. "Meantime, then, I expect I'll need to ask you where I can find a hotel for the night. And I expect I better stock up on some eatables for my saddlebags." Somehow this morning he seemed to have forgotten all of his travelling supplies and left the whole kaboodle with the Wright family.

"Beans and bacon I can take care of, friend, but

76

we don't have a hotel hereabouts. Miz Jordan takes in boarders, though, if they don't smell too ripe and she likes the way they ask."

"Fair enough again," Longarm said, "and I appreciate the advice. I'll hold my hat in both hands and act polite when I ask her."

He made his purchases, paid for with cash instead of a voucher that would have given him away, and got directions to Mrs. Jordan's place.

Longarm held his hat in his hands, talked as politely as he knew how, and was granted the favor of a room from Mrs. Jordan. She turned out to be a heavyset, powerful-looking woman in her late fifties or early sixties who was almost as tall as Longarm and probably outweighed him by sixty pounds—and not all of that difference was fat. Longarm was glad that arm-wrestling was not necessary for admission to the room, because the woman just might have whipped him. Aside from her size, she looked half mean. There was nothing of the jolly plump person in her.

"Twenty-five cents for the room," she stated briskly. "That includes the breakfast but no supper. Supper I cook for my man only. You go someplace else for that. You come in tonight drunk and I don't open the door for you. After ten o'clock the door stays locked no matter how you come home. No excuses."

"Yes, ma'am," Longarm said meekly.

She showed him the way to a clean if rather spartan room and stood with folded arms inspecting him while he put his things in the wardrobe.

When she went on about her business downstairs, Longarm poured a basin of water and washed, then brushed his clothing, ready to go out. He was hungry after spending most of the day in the saddle, and he had not been carrying food this time, so he was overdue for his lunch.

"Remember," Mrs. Jordan said as he went down to the front door, "ten o'clock, mister."

"Yes, ma'am."

There was a cafe of sorts attached to the smaller of Holyoke's general stores. It seemed to be the only place in town, so Longarm decided it looked like a right nice place to have a meal. He was almost right. It was a place to have a meal.

The coffee was too rank to be worth lingering over, so he ate quickly, paid, and left.

He stopped on the street and leaned against the storefront wall of the mercantile to light a cheroot and wonder how to pass the time until supper—which hardly promised to be a highlight of the day—and then bed.

He considered a nap. Lord knew, he had gotten little enough sleep last night. But he was not accustomed to sleeping during the day. The prospect held no appeal.

There was the town's one saloon across the street. With luck, they might stock something worth putting in a man's stomach. He ambled over there.

There were two men at the bar with tall, foamy glasses of beer before them. No card games were in progress at this time of day, although there were several tables waiting for the evening's play. Longarm joined the crowd at the bar.

"What'll it be?" the barman asked.

"Rye whiskey," Longarm said. "Out of Maryland if you have it."

"Pennsylvania do?"

"Only if that's as close as you can come."

"Pennsylvania rye, Kentucky blend, Jamaica rum, or the trade whiskey that I put together my own self."

"Rye, please," Longarm said. He knew better than to ask the man what went into the trade whiskey. The fellow might tell him, and it was probably better not to know.

The barman brought the bottle, an unfamiliar shape and label, and deposited it and a very small shot glass on the bar. Longarm laid a silver dollar on the bar beside the bottle and said, "Tally it up when I'm done."

The bartender nodded and went back to polishing glasses.

Longarm tried a shot of the whiskey. It was rye and it warmed his stomach, smoothing out the rough edges left over from a greasy lunch. That was about all he could say for it.

The two other men at the bar had been talking quietly. Now one of them turned toward Longarm. "You're new in town." It was not a question.

"Uh-huh."

"Stage ain't in yet."

"Not that I know of," Longarm agreed.

The man grunted and turned back toward his companion. He leaned close to the second man and whispered something in the fellow's ear, which drew a snort of laughter from both of them.

Longarm ignored them and poured himself another drink. The second tasted a little better than the first one had.

He leaned an elbow on the bar, turning so that he was facing the two others.

There was something vaguely familiar about the one who had spoken to him.

Longarm searched his memory, but he could not come up with anything. He was fairly sure after a few minutes that he had never seen the man before. Yet . . .

He shook his head. He could not remember. If there was anything to remember, it would probably come to him in time. He had another shot of the Pennsylvania whiskey.

After a while he collected his change from the barman and wandered off.

He bought a Denver *Post* from the larger general store and found a bench to sit on while he read. It was not until he was comfortably settled, with a cheroot in the corner of his mouth and his boots crossed at the ankle, that he realized he had just paid two cents for the same edition of the newspaper that he had already read the other morning down in Wray.

Luck, Longarm thought. If he had to depend on luck to finish this case, he might be in a hell of a fix. Good thing it was such an easy one.

He had already read everything in the paper except the want ads. So he sat in the shade of the porch overhang in front of the general store and read those. He did not learn much except that he was not being cheated on his room rent compared with what was being offered elsewhere lately, and that if he wanted to buy himself a horse or a cow or a driving rig he had plenty to choose from. It was almost a shame that he did not yearn for any of those things.

Eventually the shadows lengthened enough to justify supper. The choices were still limited to a selection between one and none, so he went back to the same place where he had had lunch.

Supper was better than lunch had been—it would have been difficult for it to have been worse—and the apple pie they served for dessert was excellent. Best of all, the coffee was fresh and hot. Longarm spent as much time over the meal as he could. By the time he was done, dusk had faded into full darkness, and the stores of Holyoke had closed for the night.

Longarm yawned and stretched and lighted a cheroot, intending it to be the last of the evening. Mrs. Jordan had not said anything about the smell of cigar smoke, but it probably bothered her and he did not want to get into a fuss with the woman. The danger there was that it might turn physical, and then he would lose for sure.

Grinning to himself and more than ready to make up for the sleep he had lost to Melba Wright, he headed slowly back toward Mrs. Jordan's house. He did not bother to check his watch. He had hours to go before the 10:00 P.M. lock-out time.

He passed in front of the large general store, ambling slowly along, making no noise although he was not consciously attempting to walk quietly.

He stopped at the corner of the store building, his senses quickened by an unexpected noise from the alley between the store and the barbershop next door.

Someone was in the alley. He heard a distinct scrape of metal against metal, then the muffled hiss of a whisper.

A whisper meant that there were at least two people in the alley. After dark. Trying to be quiet.

Interesting, Longarm thought. He scratched his stomach idly with the fingers of his right hand, then reached the few additional inches to take a grip on the big revolver and slide it free of his holster.

He could still hear the soft scratch of metal on metal. The sound was something he had heard before, but not too often. It took him a moment to identify it. Then he was sure.

Someone in the alley was hard at work trying to pick a lock.

Longarm looked to his left, toward the buildings across the street. There were no streetlights in Holyoke, but lamplight came from several windows fronting the street. If he stepped into this end of the alley, the burglars would be sure to spot him against that light.

Colt still in hand, Longarm turned and slipped quietly along the front of the building.

An alley, he reflected, had two ends. He hoped the boys in the alley were keeping a close watch on the street.

Chapter 7

He moved slowly, much more concerned with being quiet than being quick. He had time. If they had succeeded in picking the lock and entering the store before he got there, well, he would wait for them to come out again. What went up must come down; what went in must come out. The idea was to surprise them, and to do that he would have to out-quiet them.

He reached the rear corner of the building next to the alley and stopped there to listen, Colt poised for a quick shot if that should become necessary. There were, after all, *some* occasions when speed was more important than silence.

He heard nothing. Still taking his time, Longarm removed his Stetson and held it out of the way in his left hand. He made sure of his grip on the smooth, solid butt of the Colt with his right hand, squatted low, and peered around the corner of the building.

The alley was empty save for some discarded bottles and boxes and other pieces of unidentifiable trash. There was nothing of interest now between him and the faint light from across the street.

Longarm stood, moving with less hesitation now. He replaced his Stetson on his head and reached inside his coat for a cheroot. Smoke would give him away, but he could have the pleasure of chewing on it while he waited. He tugged the hatbrim lower and shifted around the corner into the alley. Back against the outside wall of the mercantile, he moved sideways until he was near the door. He could see now that the lock had been successfully picked; the door stood a few inches ajar.

Longarm smiled grimly and leaned back against the building with his arms folded, the dark steel of the Colt an extension of his right hand, supported comfortably on his left forearm. He mouthed the wrapper of the cheroot and waited.

They did not take long inside. They must have already looked the place over, probably while posing as customers, and knew what they wanted and where to find it. While they were inside he heard no whispering or stumbling, either.

Reasonably professional about it, Longarm concluded. And the average cowpuncher would not likely be able to pick a turnbolt lock. From where he stood, Longarm could not see what brand of lock had been installed by the pleasant, helpful man who ran the store, but it looked like a good strong one.

He thought about that and did some remembering until he heard a faint creak of board flooring inside to tell him that the unwelcome visitors were returning.

A couple, a man and a pregnant woman, crossed the mouth of the alley, thirty or forty feet away. They did not have any reason to look into the alley and continued on their way without seeing Longarm lurking there.

The burglars reached the door and Longarm shifted the unlighted cheroot to the other side of his jaw. The thin, grim smile was back on his tanned face.

"Careful of the step down," a voice whispered. "Don't drop nothing now."

"You be careful yourself," a second man returned in a louder whisper.

"Shhhh."

Two of them, Longarm thought. He moved a few feet farther away from the door to give them room to get out before they saw him. He wanted them well clear of the door if at all possible. It was much easier to take a man in an open alley than to have to go in and dig him out of a dark and unfamiliar place at night.

The first of them appeared, his arms wrapped around some bulky object. He had to turn sideways to go through the door. His back was to Longarm.

The second one was carrying a cloth sack that bulged with the corners of small, angular objects inside.

There was enough light behind him from the street for Longarm to see and to recognize his silhouette. It was the same man who had spoken to him in the saloon that afternoon.

This was the one who had used the lockpick, Longarm was sure. Old scraps of memory came together to focus on a bit of paper seen months ago and many miles away.

He waited, letting the man pull the store door shut and jiggle the knob slightly to make sure the lock had re-set.

He heard a snicker. "Old bastard won't never be able to figger out what happened to his stuff," the burglar whispered.

"Wrong, Eddie," Longarm said in a normal speaking voice. "I'll snitch on you."

Both men froze. They were standing with their backs to the voice in the night. He had them cold.

Just to make sure there was no doubt about what could happen, Longarm thumbed the hammer of the Colt. Eddie Bright's companion flinched. Longarm did not know who the second man was, but he likely was the same man who had been with Bright in the saloon.

"Who . . . ?"

"The long arm of the law, Eddie," Longarm said.

"Shit," Bright said.

"Yeah," Longarm said agreeably. "Who'd ever have thought it, in a little burg like this. But here we all are, old son. So set your stuff down easy, one of you at a time, and then we'll go through the formalities with the cuffs and all that."

"Shit," Bright repeated.

Longarm's voice and his attitude hardened. "Put it down," he ordered. "Now."

Bright's companion moved to comply first. He knelt and gently lowered his burden to the ground. Longarm could see now that he had been carrying a crate, although what the thing contained it was impossible to see.

"Thank you," he said. "Your turn next, Eddie."

Bright, his back still toward the lawman, nodded and bent over.

Longarm did not notice immediately that Bright was bending over much further than was necessary, and he cursed himself later for that lapse.

Bright bent low and set the sack down. Still low to the ground, he lunged forward.

His right hand shot out and grabbed his companion by the belt.

Bright hauled his friend toward Longarm, using the man as an anchor post to pull himself forward and help launch him into a hard run for the street.

The friend fell sprawling between Longarm and Bright, yelling with surprise and fear as he went down in a tangle of thrashing arms and legs while his good buddy Eddie Bright raced away for freedom.

The man rolled into Longarm's legs, momentarily slowing pursuit.

Longarm kicked his way clear of the fallen companion and, ignoring him, chased after Bright.

Eddie darted onto the street and around the corner of the store building before Longarm could snap a shot at him.

Besides, damn it, there were people, innocent people, in those buildings across the way.

Longarm charged out of the mouth of the alley and brought the Colt up.

Son of a *bitch*, Longarm thought.

The couple that had walked past a moment ago were still on the sidewalk. They would be in his direct line of fire if he shot at Bright now.

He held his fire and began to run again.

Bright obviously knew the advantage he had. The couple heard the thud of boots behind them and stopped to turn and look. Bright lowered his shoulder and charged into the husband, bowling the unsuspecting fellow out of the way.

The wanted man snaked an arm out, grabbing the woman around the waist and spinning her around.

He stopped there, shielded by the woman's bulging body, and drew a small nickel-plated revolver from his coat pocket. He waved the little gun nervously in Longarm's direction.

Longarm stopped too. He stood planted in the open, square in the middle of the sidewalk, and let his breathing settle.

"Any closer, man, and I'll shoot this here woman. You know I'll do it."

Her husband, on his hands and knees and only now beginning to realize what was happening, went pale and began to beg. Longarm did not have time at the moment to pay attention to him.

"Listen to me, Eddie," Longarm said calmly. "You're a burglar, not a killer. There's paper out on you already. You're going in, Eddie, but the difference is between a five-year stretch in prison or stretching your neck. If you hurt the lady, Eddie, you'll hang. Or worse. Think about that, Eddie. Hurt her and you don't have any more protection from her, Eddie. Hurt her, and I'll burn you myself. I'll gutshoot you, Eddie. It will take you a long time to die if I do that. But if you throw that idiot little gun away and give yourself up, all you're looking at is five years."

Eddie Bright's answer was a gunshot. The little revolver fired with a report that was more a snap than a roar. Flame lanced nastily from its muzzle, but the pipsqueak slug did not come close enough for Longarm to hear its passage. The distance between them was exceptionally long for a small-caliber revolver in the hands of a nervous man who was not accustomed to guns or to gunfighting. Only sheer, lousy luck would endanger Longarm at that range, he knew. He was counting on that.

"Four shots left, Eddie."

"Five!" Bright yelled.

"Bullshit," Longarm said pleasantly. Then, remembering, he added, "Begging your pardon, ma'am. I shouldn't have said that."

Her answer was to begin to cry.

"What is that, Eddie? One of those little bitty Smiths? Or an Ivor Johnson? Doesn't matter, does it? They're both five-shot models."

Bright was illuminated by lamplight from a window at his side. Longarm could see that he was scared and sweating. He was blinking rapidly, and his gun hand was trembling. Eddie Bright was in this way the hell over his head.

"Five years, Eddie. Or a real ugly death. Take your pick, old son."

"Who are you?" Bright's voice was shaky too.

"Deputy United States marshal," Longarm told him calmly.

"Aw, Jesus." Bright fired again, although Longarm suspected he had not intended to. This time chance sent the bullet plowing into the boards of the sidewalk a good five feet in front of Longarm and a yard to his right.

"It's just five years," Longarm said patiently. "You're a young man yet. Let the lady go and give yourself up."

The lady in question was undeniably terrified. She looked as pale as her husband and began to clutch at her swollen belly.

"Three more shots, Eddie. Then what do you do?"

Bright fired again. Longarm had no idea where that slug went.

"Two more, Eddie, and you're out of luck. If you had a dozen more it wouldn't matter. You aren't good enough to hit me this far out. But this big old thing of mine can pick the buttons off your coat if I want to use it. Think about that, Eddie."

The woman's legs gave out. She was not being clever. She had fainted dead away.

Eddie Bright was not strong enough to continue to hold her dead weight in front of him, and he was not bright enough to drop to the sidewalk with her when she slumped down out of his grasp.

He stood there, petrified, looking at Longarm with wide-eyed fear.

Longarm relaxed. "Drop the gun, Eddie, and—"

His orders were interrupted by a string of fire-cracker explosions from beside Eddie Bright.

Jesus! Longarm thought.

The husband had a little hideout gun, too, very much like Eddie Bright's.

Now that his wife was out of the way, the man simply pointed the gun and emptied it into Eddie Bright's side.

Longarm felt a hollow ache deep in his gut. "You didn't have to do that," he said in a voice so soft it was almost a whisper. "It was under control, damn it."

He ran forward. The husband's little gun was empty. Longarm plucked it from his fingers and tossed it aside to make sure the fool would not do any more damage with it, then bent over Eddie Bright. The husband was already taking care of the woman.

"Am I dyin'?"

"Yes." Longarm picked up Eddie's revolver and dropped it into his pocket.

Bright looked frightened. He tried to force a smile. "I almost made it, didn't I, Deputy?"

"You almost did," Longarm lied. "You had me

buffaloed, Eddie. It was just the other fella you didn't count on."

"Yeah. Almos' made it." Bright coughed once, and the spark of life left his eyes, leaving them glassy and empty.

Longarm stood. He looked down at the man who was solicitously trying to help his wife to her feet. He thought about saying something to the man. What he *wanted* to do was kick the ignorant fool in the face, but that would accomplish nothing. People like that likely were incapable of learning anyway, Longarm sometimes thought.

He turned and ran back toward the alley, certain he would find it empty.

Instead, incredibly, he found the second burglar still there, cowering on the ground with his face buried in his arms. The man—he was hardly more than a boy, and for an instant Longarm was reminded of Tim Wright—was crying.

Longarm hauled him to his feet, checked him for weapons, and handcuffed him. He was unarmed unless you would count a Barlow knife with a cracked handle.

Longarm sighed. So much for his plan to take a look at the Simmons Express Company without anyone knowing he was a deputy. That had certainly been blown all to hell and gone.

He took his prisoner back out onto the street to look for whatever passed as the law locally and to find the owner of the store that had just been robbed. Whatever was in that box and the sack that had been stolen needed to be put back under lock and key before someone else made off with it.

Chapter 8

There was no local law in Holyoke, so Longarm still had his prisoner in the morning. The young man's name was Harley Caddell. He was twenty years old, and Eddie Bright had been his cousin. The burglary of Roland Petersen's store, he swore, had been the very first job he had *ever* gone on with Eddie. Longarm was frankly unsure whether to believe him or not. Certainly the kid had not acquitted himself like a seasoned lawbreaker. On the other hand, people who commit burglaries are not nice folks. Some of them have even been known to lie.

Regardless, young Caddell would be someone else's problem just as soon as Longarm could get him to Julesburg.

Longarm got two tickets on the morning northbound run to Julesburg. Petersen refused to accept payment or even a federal voucher for the fares.

"No, sir, Marshal Long. No way am I going to let you pay anything after what you did for me last night." The storekeeper gave Caddell a hard look. The kid flinched away from it and would not again look Petersen in the eyes.

Bright and Caddell had been making off with firearms, jewelry, practically everything Petersen had in his store that was small, light, easily transportable, and of value.

"Your money just is no good in my store, Marshal," Petersen insisted.

Longarm thanked him and accepted the pair of pasteboard tickets.

A lean, bearded man entered the store. The fellow wore a slouch hat and a linen duster and carried a long whip coiled in one hand. If he was armed, Longarm could not see any evidence of it because of the duster. Petersen smiled and beckoned the man to them.

"I got someone here you have to meet, Royce," he said. "Marshal Custis Long, this here is Royce Hapwell. Royce is the driver of the Simmons coach. You'll be riding with him today. Royce, this gentleman is a deputy marshal out o' Denver. He's taking a prisoner to Julesburg for jailing." Petersen pointed with his chin toward the unhappy Caddell. "The little sumbitch tried to rob me last night. Would of got away with it, too, if it hadn't been for Marshal Long here."

The deputy, half a head taller than the Simmons jehu, shook hands with Hapwell. "You can call me Longarm," he said. "I've tried to tell that to Mr. Petersen, but he won't have it."

"All right. Longarm it is." Hapwell shifted a chew from one side of his jaw to the other and looked around, but there was no cuspidor nearby. He held it. "If you can do that much for Rollie, Marshal, I sure hell hope you can do something for Miz Simmons an' her troubles."

94

"Oh? Been having troubles?"

The driver grunted. "Damn straight, we been. Robberies, Longarm. Bunch of damned armed men stopping our coach every time there's anything worth carrying. Every damn time, I tell you."

"Really?"

"Every time that I've knowed about it, anyhow."

"Tell me about it," Longarm suggested, as if it was all news to him.

Hapwell did. His story was very much the same as the Julesburg postmaster had reported, although in somewhat greater detail.

"There's always six of them, Longarm, and they always come at us out of just plain nowhere. You ain't seen the road yet, I expect, but you'll see today. There ain't hardly a place where a man could hide, but they always find a way somehow. No way I could outrun them with a bone-tired four-up like we use. And Miz Simmons, she always says for us not to put up a fight of it. Says things ain't as important as people, so when they show we're s'posed to stop the coach an' do whatever it takes to make sure the passengers don't get hurt."

Longarm found it interesting that the company's standing orders were to avoid resistance.

The postmaster had already suggested that it looked like inside information to him. Royce Hapwell made no such suggestion.

Although that, Longarm knew, could simply be a natural blind spot in his reasoning caused by loyalty to his employer.

Or it could be something else again. He would have to reserve judgement about that.

"What about guards?" Longarm asked.

"There's just me in the box," Hapwell said, "and whatever passengers we're carrying down below. Company can't afford guards." He frowned. "As of last Tuesday we don't have no insurance, neither. The carrier dropped us, an' she don't know of any others as would take us on. Not at any rates we could afford to pay, anyhow. As she stands, Longarm, I got to ask all passengers to sign a piece o' paper saying they won't hold the line responsible for any losses. If they ain't willing to sign the paper, I ain't allowed to carry them." He worked his jaw and looked a little uncomfortable. He walked across the store to find a cuspidor and spat, then returned.

"I . . . uh . . . don't suppose you'd volunteer to ride guard for me this trip?" He sounded genuinely hopeful.

"Is there anything of value going north today?"

Hapwell paused to look at Petersen with a raised eyebrow.

The storekeeper and south-end stage-line representative nodded. "Bag of deposits going to the bank in Julesburg," he said. He looked at Caddell. "Him and his pal didn't know about that, I expect."

"How many people would know about it?" Longarm asked.

Petersen shrugged. "Nobody but me and now the rest of us in here right now," he said. "I been making it a point to not let anybody know when I was going to send the bag out."

"It's your deposit, Mr. Petersen?" Longarm asked.

"Mine and just about everybody else's in Holyoke. Since we don't have a bank of our own yet, though I expect we will by and by, I collect the little bank bags here in one big poke, one of those heavy, reinforced kinds like they carry mail in, and every week or two I give them to Royce to carry to the bank for us. Then the bank mails back the deposit slips or whatever. I never know myself how much is in the sack, because I never look into anybody else's bag and they never get a peek in mine."

"So the fact that the deposit shipments are made is common knowledge in Holyoke?"

Petersen thought about that for a moment. "I expect it would be."

"How often have your deposit sacks been stolen?" Longarm asked.

The man looked surprised, and so did Hapwell.

"Come to think of it, Marshal, we haven't lost any of our money yet."

Longarm looked at the driver. "But I thought you said—"

Hapwell scratched his chin through the thick fur of his beard. "I never thought about it all that much," he said, "but all the robberies've been on the downrun. You know. From Julie down t' here."

Longarm tucked that information away to be thought about later, but the immediate implication was plain enough. Whoever was tipping the gang of robbers to their day's work, the information was coming from the Julesburg end of the route. That eliminated Petersen, but not Hapwell. It could be that Hapwell, if he were the rotten apple in the Simmons barrel, simply had no way to get in touch with his robber friends when he was down at this end of the run.

"If you want me to," Longarm said, "I'll ride shot-gun for you today."

Hapwell looked genuinely pleased to hear it. "Thank you, Longarm."

"If this man does half as much for you as he already did for me," Petersen said, "you can tell Miz Jenny that she doesn't have anything more to worry about."

"I'll tell her you said so," Hapwell said.

Longarm managed to avoid showing the annoyance he felt. He might as well have hired a brass band *and* a fife-and-drum corps to announce his arrival in Julesburg.

He took young Caddell by the elbow and led him out to the coach while Petersen got the shipping box ready for Hapwell to load in the driving boot.

There were two other passengers waiting to board, each of them with a pale square of pasteboard in her hand. Both were women, approximately in their early thirties. They were dressed normally enough for travel, but traces of powder beside their noses and an un-natural brightness high on their cheeks showed what their occupation had to be. They should have used a little more soap when they washed this morning, Longarm thought.

Still, he nodded to them politely and asked if they would mind sharing the passenger compartment with a manacled prisoner.

"Whatever you say, honey," one of them told him. The other woman elbowed her sharply in the ribs, re-minding her to watch her manners in public. Such soiled doves were virtually everywhere. In private they might be welcomed with enthusiasm, but in public they were expected to pretend a decorum that would have led them to starvation in their private performances.

"Thank you, ladies," Longarm said, playing the game. He helped them into the coach, which was a cheap, smaller substitute for the big Conestogas and Studebakers operated by more prosperous lines, and allowed them to choose their seats before he put Caddell aboard and handcuffed the youngster to a seat arm.

"If he gives you any trouble, ladies, I want you to let me know about it." He gave Caddell a hard look to underline that instruction with an unspoken warning.

"I won't do nothing, Marshal," Caddell promised.

"Up to you whether you do or not," Longarm said.

He went back inside the store to get his things and put them into the luggage rack hanging on the back of the coach. He pulled the Winchester out of its scabbard, though, and propped it in a corner of the driving box, just in case.

By the time Hapwell completed his loading and his paperwork for the run north, Longarm was ready.

Hapwell climbed into the box and picked up his lines. He shook them out and took a light contact on the horses' mouths, then released the brake.

Longarm picked up his Winchester and laid it across his lap, then reached for a cheroot. He leaned back and propped his boots against the mud guard at the front of the high box. He was honestly not sure himself if he hoped for a smooth trip north or if it might be better if the robbery gang changed their methods today and met him head-on.

Regardless of what he wanted, though, he realized, that part of it was not within his control.

Whatever happened, he would just have to be ready for it.

The drive north was uneventful, and the country here was no more thrilling than what he had been passing through farther to the south. It was depressingly like the land between Wray and Holyoke: one barren rise after another, bunchgrass and soapweed and sage, the same empty scene mile after mile after mile.

The only difference that Longarm could see was that here someone—probably the Simmons Express Company or the line that had preceded it—had erected a nearly unbroken line of snow fencing to keep the road clear when the winter snows started howling across the plains.

The plains winds could be fierce at any time of year, and when they carried snow on them drifts could pile up ten feet deep or more downwind of any obstruction, including the tops of the endless number of rises. The artificial barrier of a snow fence placed the drifts where they would do no harm and kept them off the public road.

Aside from that, though, there was little to be seen. There were few side roads, although from time to time a set of wheel ruts would veer off the roadway and wind out of sight toward some distant ranch or farmyard. Some of the side roads seemed to have been added fairly recently, at least since the snow fence was erected.

Hapwell drove past one, and Longarm yawned and looked to his right, examining the slender link between some isolated and probably impoverished dwelling and the rest of the world. Whoever had made it, almost certainly by the simple expedient of driving over it enough times to form identifiable ruts, had not even bothered to remove the fence where it crossed the road. They had simply knocked the already sagging fence down and driven over it.

While he rode, Longarm thought. Hapwell might not think so, but there were ten thousand places between Holyoke and Julesburg where a gang of robbers or a troop of cavalry or half the Sioux nation could have chosen to hide, off the road but concealed from it, certainly within an easy gallop of a passing stage.

Behind any one or behind each one of the infinite number of low rises, a man or a group of men on horseback could remain safely concealed until they chose to put in an appearance.

That, Longarm thought, was no mystery at all.

"Where do you change horses?" Longarm asked as the sun was high overhead.

"No change," Hapwell told him. The man grinned. "I know. Don't tell me. The idea of a stage is t' go it in stages, right? Move 'em fast and change 'em often. Well, that's the way they do it on the big outfits. An' we really ought to have a change midway in the trip. But there ain't no place to keep extry horses, an' Miz Simmons don't have the money to build and operate a relay point of her own. So the one team has to do all the job."

"Every day?"

Hapwell shrugged. "The line owns two teams, four head apiece. They run down one day an' back the next, then get to rest whilst the other bunch goes out. Three teams'd be better. One on the road and one waiting at each end. Four teams and a relay point in the middle would be the best of all. But that takes money."

"I see." Longarm lighted another cheroot, cupping his hand around the flare of the match to protect it from the breeze.

"Hungry?" Hapwell asked.

"A mite."

"We'll have a lunch stop in another half mile. Can't

see it from here, but there's a windmill an' stock tank we can stop at. The owner don't mind. There's no shade, but there's water and a chance to move around some. That's good for something. Say, I hope Petersen told you the line don't provide lunches. Those as wants to eat are supposed to carry their own."

"I don't believe he mentioned it."

Hapwell grunted. "I can share."

"It's all right," Longarm told him. "I have enough in my saddlebags for the prisoner and me."

"You're sure?"

Longarm nodded. "What about the . . . uh . . . ladies?"

"Them? Hell, they know. Make this run every couple weeks. Not enough business in Holyoke to keep a regular house down there, so some gals come down every so often an' pick up extra money hauling what ashes've collected since the last time they was down." He grinned and winked. "That blonde one's Lisa. Not bad."

"Thanks for the tip," Longarm said without meaning it.

He was going to question the driver more about the men in the robbery gang but was interrupted when they reached another of the turnoffs. Hapwell clucked soothingly to his team and eased them into a wide turn. They rattled across the beaten-down snow fence, over a section where the thin, weathered slats had been ground to splinters by the passage of heavy, shod hoofs, and pulled to a stop beside a galvanized steel tank and windmill. The tank had a float valve to demand water from the mill, but even so the ground around it was muddy. The tracks of cattle showed in the mud. There were boot tracks too but no indications that horses had been drinking from the tank.

Hapwell set his brake and let the weary horses slouch in their collars. He left them in harness when he climbed down and opened the coach door.

"You don't water them?" Longarm asked.

"Course I do, but I'll let them cool off first and then carry it to 'em in a bucket. Easier than breaking the hitch."

Longarm propped his Winchester in a corner of the boot and climbed down to the ground. It felt good to be able to walk around after so long on the unpadded wooden seat of the coach. Hapwell carried a pillow for himself but none for a passenger.

The whores got out, one of them carrying a small hamper. They walked off to the other side of the tank and ate standing up rather than soil their out-in-public dresses.

"Marshal?" Caddell whispered.

"Uh-huh?"

"You got to unlock me here."

"I got to?"

"Well, maybe not, but I wisht you would. I got to take a leak, Marshal. I been about to bust for the past hour."

Longarm unlocked the cuff that was around the seat arm and led the young burglar away from the coach until they were out of sight of the women. Not that it would have shocked the whores, but it would have made Longarm uncomfortable to impose the sight on any female. And he had to go too.

He returned Caddell to the coach and secured him to the seat again, then went around back to get some jerky from his saddlebags.

"Is this all you got?" the prisoner protested.

"You don't have to eat it if you don't want." Longarm held his hand out to take the meat back.

"No. This'll be just fine."

Chewing on a hunk of the tough, dried meat, Longarm went forward to where Hapwell was squatting beside one of the wheels with a thick sandwich in his hands and a slab of cold pie on a piece of brown paper beside him.

"Got plenty if you want to join me," the driver offered again.

"Thanks, but I'm fine. Is that a spare cup I saw back there?" He nodded toward the back of the coach and the luggage boot.

"Yeah, help yourself."

"Thanks." Longarm got the tin cup, rinsed it in the stock tank, and filled it. He drank from it, then filled it again and carried it to Caddell.

Caddell saw him coming. He made a face. "Water and shoe leather. Helluva way for a man to treat a prisoner. But then Eddie told me that all you lawdogs was bastards."

"Eddie was right," Longarm said agreeably. He drank off half a cup of the water, wiped his mouth with the back of his hand, and poured what remained onto the ground. He tossed the empty cup into the luggage boot and climbed back up onto the driving box.

"Hey!" Caddell hollered. "Hey, damn it!"

Longarm ignored him.

After the women had returned to the coach and the horses were watered, Hapwell climbed up beside Longarm and put the team in motion again. He pulled them around in a tight circle. The wheelers had to sidestep and the near leader step out smartly, but they made the turn in perfect coordination despite the tightness of the turn.

"Nice," Longarm commented.

Hapwell grinned. "Thanks."

"A man who can handle a team like that could get a job with just about any line, couldn't he?"

Hapwell grinned again and chuckled. "You'd think that, wouldn't you? But . . . uh, I been known to drink some. Time to time. Miz Simmons, she puts up with it. Kinda has to. She don't want to lose the only driver around who can't afford to leave her."

"I see," Longarm said.

The man shrugged. "It ain't anything you wouldn't hear in town if you was to ask."

Longarm questioned him about the robbers. Hapwell acted like a man who was freely giving all the information he knew.

He had no idea what any of them looked like. They all wore flour sacks over their heads. No hats. Holes cut out for the eyes. They used the same sacks for all the robberies. He knew that because several of them had drawn faces on their masks.

"Charcoal, it looks like they used. You know. Drawed on mouths and moustaches and the like. I'd know them masks again, straight off. But I couldn't tell you nothing about what the men look like."

The horses and the clothing were not always the same. He could not remember about the saddles they rode. The guns he did remember.

"Shotguns, Longarm. They every damn one of them carry shotguns. Helluva scary thing to be looking down the tubes of a shotgun, you know."

Longarm knew. He had done it himself, and he did not like it.

"Revolvers? You know, I purely don't recall if they had any or not. All I can remember of the guns is them big damn muzzles of the shotguns. Don't recall about rifles neither. Nothing special about their voices that I can think of. . . . No, sir, I don't have a clue about how old they might be. Not any of them. But one of 'em has a belly that kind of spreads down over his belt buckle. I expect he could be older, or just fat. Hard to tell when you can't see nothing of the face or hair."

They reached Julesburg—and the railroad, and civilization—late in the afternoon.

Longarm gathered up his gear and his prisoner and went to find the local sheriff so he could be relieved of the burden of Harley Caddell.

Chapter 9

Longarm was having an early breakfast the next morning when Royce Hapwell found him and took a seat across the table from him without waiting for an invitation. "How's it going, Longarm?"

The tall deputy shrugged. "Busy day today. Everybody I wanted to see was already closed up and gone by the time I got my prisoner turned over to your sheriff last night."

Hapwell grinned. "What did you think of our sheriff?"

Longarm grunted somthing that might have meant anything, and Hapwell laughed. "Yeah," the coach driver said. "That's what everybody else thinks 'bout him too."

"Well," Longarm said diplomatically, "I will say that he doesn't seem to have any objections to an outsider coming in here and claiming jurisdiction."

Hapwell chuckled. "Bet he'd turn the whole county over to you if you was to ask nice. Long as old Max got to keep the badge an' the salary for the job."

Longarm did not respond to that. Very often the feeling was that it was all right for one of the home folks to criticize their own, but that same invitation was not extended to visitors. "Coffee?" he asked.

Hapwell shook his head. "I ate better'n an hour ago, but I thank you. I already got the rig ready to roll south again."

"I take it you had something particular in mind when you looked me up, then?"

"Uh-huh. The boss lady wanted me to find you and bring you over to the office."

Longarm looked at his plate. He had barely begun to get into his meal.

"She'll be there all morning. I could tell her you'll come later, if you want," Hapwell said.

"If you wouldn't mind," Longarm said.

"Sure thing. You won't forget?"

"I already had it in mind to meet her today."

"All right, I'll tell her."

"You do that, Royce."

The stage driver left, and Longarm took his time about finishing his meal. He paid for it, lighted a cheroot, and pulled the Ingersol from his vest pocket. The post office should be open now, and he wanted to stop there first. After all, it was the postmaster and not the Simmons Express Company that had turned in the report to Marshal Vail's office about the robberies.

He found the post office without difficulty and was taken immediately to the postmaster's private office.

The man was a political appointee, of course, but he seemed to be trying to perform his duties in a professional manner. The employees that Longarm saw were both courteous and efficient, which was not all that common in government offices.

"Thanks for coming, Deputy Long," the postmaster said when they were introduced. "I'm Norman Bentley. I received a wire from Marshal . . . uh . . . Vail?"

Longarm nodded, confirming that Bentley had remembered the name correctly.

"Yes. Thank you. He said that you would be along."

Longarm made a mental note to remember to send a telegram to Billy.

"Now. What may I do for you, Deputy?"

"You can tell me if you know anything about this case beyond what was in the report you already sent to Denver, Mr. Bentley. Anything at all."

"Unfortunately, Deputy, you already know virtually everything I am sure of and much of what I surmise." The postmaster smiled. "Which may not be much. I have never claimed great powers of deduction, you see. Unlike you field men. I rather envy you, you know."

"There's times when you might not," Longarm said, thinking of the living conditions that were sometimes required.

"I'm sure," Bentley said with polite disbelief.

"You mentioned in your report that it looks like an inside deal, sir," Longarm said, turning the conversation to the business that had brought him here.

Bentley spread his hands. "An example of the simplest sort of deductive reasoning, Deputy. The robberies happen only when there is something worth stealing on the coach. And the mail pouch is never disturbed unless there is registered material included."

"Do you take special precautions with the registered mail, Mr. Bentley?"

The postmaster looked offended. "Of course we do, Deputy. Of course."

"For instance?"

"Registered materials are required to be carried in special containers, reinforced that is, with double locks. First-class mail can travel under a single lock."

"When there's both registered and first-class mail, do they go together in the same bag?"

"Yes. It would be pointless to pay for the shipment of two parcels. We do, of course, separate the different classes of materials within the shipping container. They travel in separate pouches within a common container."

"Uh-huh," Longarm mused. "Mind if I smoke?"

"Please do." Bentley leaned forward and turned a humidor on his desk to face Longarm. The cigars he offered were plump, pale, obviously expensive items. Longarm was tempted but declined. Having a nickel cigar habit was bad enough without developing a taste for something really expensive.

Both men lit up. They talked some more, but Bentley honestly had included virtually everything in his report. Mail had been stolen from the Simmons coaches on two separate occasions.

"You don't happen to know offhand just how many times the Simmons Company has been hit, do you?" Longarm asked.

Bentley thought about that for a moment. "One hears talk, of course, but I am only certain of those instances that have involved mail losses. I would say, oh, half a dozen robberies in addition to those during which mail was stolen." He paused. "That would be an approximate figure, of course."

"So they didn't bother the mail those other times," Longarm said.

"No. Only twice, as I reported to Marshal Vail."

"You didn't file a report after the first instance," Longarm noted.

"Immediately following the first robbery," Bentley said, "I reported to the local authorities. That experience prompted me to go through federal government channels when the loss was repeated."

Longarm did not pursue that. He did not need to. He already had the opinion he was likely to keep about the local sheriff. The only surprise was that Bentley had bothered to file a report with the man after the first robbery. Likely, Longarm thought, they belonged to the same political party, and Bentley was trying to keep fences from needing mending.

Longarm stood and extended his hand. Bentley rose, and they shook.

"Thank you, sir. I appreciate your help," Longarm said.

"If there is anything I can do, Deputy, anything at all . . ."

"Yes, sir. Thank you."

He left the post office and walked to the Union Pacific railroad depot, remembering for a change to submit an in-progress report to Billy.

He wondered if Vail would fall off his chair in shock and amazement when that wire hit his desk. Longarm enjoyed speculating on the possibility.

He asked directions next to the Simmons Express Company offices and even so had some difficulty finding it. The Simmons outfit was housed in a ramshackle barn at the south edge of Julesburg, nearly a quarter of a mile beyond the last residences of the town. The courthouse roof and the flag and pole outside the post office were barely visible from it, past the roofs of the houses in between and a very few treetops. There were no stores or other businesses in sight of the barn. Except for the houses, lined up neatly along an obviously planned and surveyed street,

111

the only major building in sight was a schoolhouse with its distinctive bell tower.

It was not a convenient location and seemed a sure sign of the company's lack of prosperity. Its isolation from town would present a serious drawback for both passenger and freight traffic. Longarm had not noticed if Julesburg had a formal hackney service, but that or some impromptu substitute would be necessary to transport people and parcels from the railroad depot for shipment down to Holyoke by the Simmons Company.

Longarm could not help wondering as he walked the last hundred yards to the barn if the company was so broke it was having to make ends meet by stealing from its own customers.

He gnawed on the stub of the cigar he had started in Bentley's office and thought about that.

So far the company had not experienced any financial losses from the string of robberies. According to Hapwell, they had had insurance coverage until this past week. And now they were asking passengers and shippers to sign waivers so the company would not be responsible for losses to the highwaymen.

That being the case, Longarm reasoned, it was entirely conceivable that the operators of the stage line themselves could be providing that inside information.

He threw away the cigar butt and lengthened his stride for the last few paces to the sun-bleached slab sides of the old barn.

A gray-haired old jasper whose face was dotted with dirty white beard stubble was washing down a horse just outside the wide front doors of the barn. Longarm recognized the horse as one of the wheelers of the team that had brought him up from Holyoke the day before.

The old fellow paused from his chore when Long-arm arrived.

"Good morning," Longarm said pleasantly. "Where could I find the office?"

"Inside an' just to yer right. Used t' to be the harness room. Office now."

"Thanks." Longarm went inside.

A moment later, he stepped back into the sunshine. "I thought you said . . ."

"You ast where the office was. I told you. Did you ask where the lady was I'd of told you that." He picked up the bucket of water he had been dipping his rag into and sloshed the rest of it over the big animal's back, then set it aside and took up a scraper that he would use to remove most of the water from the horse's coat.

"All right," Longarm said patiently. "Where's Mrs. Simmons?"

"Gone." The man went on with his work.

"I thought she was going to be here all morning."

"Don't know anything about gonna be or s'posed t' be," the man said. "Don't know where she went, neither. She didn' say. Said she'd be back after dinner."

"Thank you."

"You're welcome." He stopped and gave Longarm a close inspection. The whites of his eyes were yellowed. He did not look healthy, but he acted spry enough for his age. "You'd be the marshal?"

"Uh-huh."

"Long, is it?"

"Most call me Longarm."

"You wanta know who's doing the robbing?"

"That's why I came here."

The old man sniffed, though whether that was a comment or a head cold Longarm could not quite tell. "It don't take no figuring to know that, son."

"Really?"

"Course not." The old boy sounded positive.

"I'd appreciate any help you might be able to give me," Longarm said.

He sniffed again. Longarm still was not sure how to take that.

"Is there a ree-ward?"

"None that I know of, unless the stage company has posted one. There hasn't been time enough for the post office to make a decision like that."

"Huh!" The old fellow sniffed again. This time Longarm was reasonably sure it was derision rather than congestion that caused it. "Miz Simmons can't afford wages, hardly. She ain't gonna be posting no ree-wards."

"I'd still appreciate your help if you have any ideas about who is behind the holdups," Longarm said.

"Yeah, well, wait a bit."

Longarm waited while the old man finished removing the worst of the water from the horse's back and belly. He tossed the scraper into the empty bucket and led the animal into a small corral that was newer and considerably stouter than the barn, then turned it loose in the sun to dry. Another of yesterday's team was already there, so apparently the old fellow was halfway through his morning's work.

"Come inside, young fellow," the old man said when he returned. "An' by the way, you can call me Hands."

"Hans?" Longarm repeated, giving the pronunciation a German twist.

"Nope. Hands." He held out his hands and showed them to Longarm. They were gnarly and twisted. "Used to have the best hands on a set of driving lines that anybody ever seen, if I do say so myself." His hands now looked like so many claws protruding from a lump of tissue. "Can't tell it now, but they used to was," Hands said.

"Rheumatism?" Longarm asked.

"Huh. If it was only that, I'd still be drivin'. No, some jealous sons of bitches got me down one night and stomped me. Laid my hands onto a chunk o' stovewood an' put the boots to 'em. Ain't been worth a shit since." He cackled and added, "Sons o' bitches knew I'd never be able to use a gun agin, but they forgot I might still be able to hang onta the end of an axe handle. Done it, too, quick as I healed up. Sons of bitches."

He led the way inside the Simmons Company office and flopped into the swivel chair behind the desk, leaving a straight-backed chair for Longarm to use. "You can smoke in here if you want. Don't allow it in the rest o' the place, o' course, but it's all right in here."

Longarm thanked him and pulled out a cheroot. He offered one to Hands, suspecting that the information had been as much hint as it was permission. Hands took the cheroot and accepted a light from Longarm as well. He leaned back in the swivel chair.

"You want me to tell you who done the robbing, huh?"

"Yes, I do," Longarm said.

Hands squinted at him for a moment, then turned

away. He leaned down and dug under a pile of empty feed sacks against the wall behind the desk. When he straightened up again he had a bottle in one twisted hand. "Nip?"

"Don't mind if I do," Longarm said.

Hands used the few teeth he had left to remove the cork. He peered at the bottle, which was nearly empty, and spat the cork onto the floor. Obviously he expected to empty it. Almost as obviously, Longarm thought, he knew who would be expected to replace it with a full one.

Cheap at the price, Longarm thought, if Hands really did have any information that would be useful.

Hands took a swallow for himself and passed the bottle to Longarm. Longarm drank only sparingly. The liquor was awful, but Hands seemed to enjoy it.

"Ahhh," Hands said with feeling. He grinned and said, "Does wonders for the rheumatiz, it does." He drank again.

"I thought you said . . ."

"Pay *attention,* son. I said it wasn't rheumatiz that done for my hands. I never said I didn't have it."

"Oh." Longarm realized he was just going to have to wait the old fellow out if he wanted to hear what Hands had to say.

The old boy took another swallow and gave the bottle to Longarm, who made a show of drinking, but was careful to let damned little of the nauseating stuff enter his mouth.

Hands finished the bottle and tucked the empty evidence out of sight beneath the feed sacks again. He sighed once and belched. "Now, son, what was it you wanted to know?"

"About the robberies?"

"Oh, yeah. Them." Hands tilted his head and squinted toward Longarm as if inspecting him. "You look old enough, maybe, if you was a kid at the time, but I don't believe you been in this part o' the country long. Is that right?"

"I'm afraid so," Longarm agreed. "I've been through a time or two before, but I couldn't say that I know it."

"You wasn't here afore the War, was you?"

Longarm shook his head.

"If you was, it'd be plain as plain can be who's behind these robberies, boy."

Longarm suppressed a smile. It had been a hell of a long time since anyone had called him "boy." "I still don't know what you mean."

"Slade, boy." Hands paused for emphasis and leaned forward in his chair. One word at a time, he breathed, "Black . . . Jack . . . Slade." He sat back in his chair with a look of triumph and folded his arms. Obviously he believed that he had just solved everything.

"I'm sorry, Hands, but I don't believe I know that name. I'm fairly sure I haven't seen it on any Wanted posters."

"You don't know 'bout Black Jack *Slade*, boy? Don't you know *nothing?*"

"Not about Slade, I'm afraid."

Hands shook his head in disbelief. "It's a pure wonder they let you loose from Denver, Deppity. A pure wonder." He leaned forward again.

"Let me tell you 'bout Black Jack Slade, son, who was certain-damn-teed the toughest, meanest, crankiest son of a pure bitch that ever forked a horse, fucked a hoor, or gutshot a man. . . ."

Chapter 10

Back during the old days, according to Hands, back
before the coming of the railroad, Julesburg had been
a division point for the Overland Stage Company, just
as it was now a division point for the Union Pacific.
The impact of the Overland Company then had been
much the same as the railroad now, in fact. The company had been the lifeblood of very nearly everything
between Missouri and the California gold fields.

A few years before the War between the States,
the Overland Company's division manager had been
a man named Joseph Slade, better known as Black
Jack.

"Lordy, he was one tough son of a bitch," Hands
said with obvious admiration. "Clean out a saloon by
his lonesome if he took the notion. An' he took the
notion fairly regular. He was tough an' he liked to
show it where everybody could see. Times he didn't
have a reason to fight, he'd go an' invent one."

Aside from being so deliberately abrasive in nature,
Slade's reputation suffered when rumors began to cir-

culate that he was the man responsible for a string of stagecoach robberies that was plaguing the Overland line at the time.

The robberies consistently occurred within a day's run from Julesburg. And the gang of robbers always seemed to know in advance when there was a valuable cargo aboard.

"Though mind you, sonny, the coaches then was carryin' the real goods. Wasn't no railroad then to haul safes and passels of guards along. Did you want to send somethin' like cash or gold from Californy to New York, or t'other way to, you either sent 'er by ship, which might well go down at sea, or you shipped 'er by the Overland. Them was the only choices."

Longarm began to have an idea of where the story was taking him.

Few shipments of any appreciable value, though, were getting past Julesburg at the time. Suspicion quite naturally fell onto Slade, who was one of the few men in the area in a position to know what was being transported on a given coach, and who was becoming quite thoroughly detested anyway for his habit of breaking limbs for his evening diversions.

The rumors turned to suspicions and those turned into open accusations when Slade was braced by an Overland supervisor named Jules Bene.

"Black Jack didn't take a hell of a lot to being named like that. He reached for his belly gun, but damned if that Bene fella wasn't faster to get his out. Not only got it out, he put the thing t' work too. Emptied the son of a bitch in old Black Jack, he did. But he went an' made one mistake. He emptied his gun inta Black Jack, but he never walked up on 'im and put a finisher inta him. Bene just walked away.

120

An' Black Jack, he didn't die from it."

Hands chuckled and added, "I said ol' Black Jack was a tough son of a bitch, an' I wasn't lying. An' I swear this is the truth. He took five slugs from a Colt's Patent .36 caliber *ree*-volver and lived to tell about it."

Longarm had heard of stranger things. But not often. Still, it was entirely possible, especially since Hands did not specify exactly where those five lead slugs had struck.

"Black Jack was through with the Overland Company, o' course, but he wasn't through with Jules Bene. After he healed up, which took considerable time, he come back an' looked up old Jules.

"Found him an' grabbed him. Black Jack and some of his friends. But nobody knows to this day 'xactly *who* helped." Hands chuckled again. Longarm thought the sound more of a cackle than a chuckle.

"Carried Jules out of town a piece an' propped him up against a telegraph pole." The old man squinted at Longarm and cocked his head to the side. "Didn't know we had such newfangled things back then, did you, boy? Well, we did. Folks out this way've always prided themselves on bein' on top o' the modern things.

"Anyway, boy, they put old Jules up against this telegraph pole an' tied his hands around back of it, so's he couldn't go anywhere. Then Black Jack, he backed off a bit an' took out his gun. They say he was gettin' considerable pleasure out of it. An' that Jules Bene was so scared he shit his pants. For sure they had to clean him up before they buried him after.

"Far as I know nobody ever could count the number of balls Slade put inta Bene that day, but he musta had to reload plenty, because Bene was tore up pretty bad before he finally got around to dyin'. Shot him here an' shot him there an' then reloaded an' shot him some more.

"Time they found Bene and brought him in there was an ear missin' off the side of his head too. Coulda been shot off, o'course, but they said afterward that when Black Jack turned up in the Montana gold country later on he was sportin' a watch fob made of leather. An' they say that watch fob looked like a human person's ear." Hands grinned. "Or so they say."

"And you think Black Jack Slade is back in the country," Longarm asked, "up to his old tricks?"

Hands grinned again. "Didn't say that, boy. Naw, word was that Slade got hisself hung up around Virginia City. By a vigilance committee, of which we heard they had a humdinger up there in those days. But I couldn't swear to that, aye or nay. What I suspicion 'bout this here situation, boy, is that either it's Black Jack Slade come home in his late years or it's one o' the boys that used to work with him on all those robberies, come back the same way."

Longarm smoothed the ends of his moustache and chewed on the stub of his cheroot. "You used to work for the Overland Company, didn't you, Hands?"

"I'm real proud to say that I did, boy."

"Here?"

Hands nodded.

"Back when Slade was the division manager?"

Hands laughed. "You think it's *me,* boy? You think I'm the one settin' up these robberies?"

Longarm shrugged.

Hands laughed again. "I told you, boy, I'm proud o' having handled the lines o' the Julesburg stage back when that there was a thing to be proud about. An' sure,

122

I was in this country back then. I was an Overland jehu, as good as ever they had. An' yeah, I worked for Black Jack Slade at the time. Worked for Jules Bene too, fer that matter. Knew 'em both. Worked for 'em both. An' never had to take any shit off either one of them. That's something you might not know about the way things was back before the railroad come, boy. Back then an Overland driver was th' cock o' the walk, boy. Nobody, including supervisors, gave any shit to an Overland driver, 'cause a man who could drive for the Overland Company could claim top dollar from anybody's outfit, an' they'd be lucky to get him.

"Did you know anything about those robberies?" Longarm asked.

"Know anything about 'em? Hell, boy, I was on the driving box more'n once when those masked sons o' bitches stopped us. Graveled my gut, too, I'll tell you. An Overland jehu then, boy, was like the captain of a tall-masted sailin' ship. Didn't have just the authority, you see. He had the responsibility too. I was the one *ree*-sponsible for my passengers an' my cargo. I took it serious. So if you're thinkin' I was any part of Slade's gang—*if* Slade was part of that gang back then, an' that still ain't been actually proven that I've ever heard tell—then, no. I had more pride than that, mister, an' I still do. I was takin' their pay, and that bought 'em more than just my time, boy. It bought the very best I had to give 'em."

"And now, Hands? What about the Simmons Express Company?"

"I'm takin' Miz Simmons's pay, boy," Hands said with quiet dignity.

Longarm nodded.

"What I was gettin' at," Hands said, "was that you

123

want to look up one of the old-timers as *was* part of Slade's gang. Or the gang that folks *said* was Slade's."

"You say Slade was hanged in Montana?"

Hands shrugged. "I heard that. I never seen it. And Lord knows, Black Jack Slade was one hard son of a bitch to kill. Jules Bene could of told you that. So I think with Black Jack I'd of had to see the body an' feel it cold before I'd believe for sure that even a hanging had took on that man."

"This was twenty years ago?" Longarm asked.

"That or a little better."

Longarm relighted what was left of his cheroot. It had gone out while he was listening to Hands. Twenty years or a bit over, he thought. A gang member who had been young at that time would still be in shape to ride and to rob. For that matter, a man who was in his forties then could still be in shape to handle a gun and a set of reins.

"How old would Slade be if he was still alive?" Longarm asked.

Hands had to think about that for a moment. "Hell, I ain't for sure. Call it . . . late fifties? early in his sixties?" He grinned. "If he was still alive, that is."

Longarm thanked Hands and stood. "I'll be back after lunch," he said. "I still need to see Mrs. Simmons."

"I'll tell her you're comin'."

Longarm thanked him again and turned to leave.

"If you see an old fart in town with a dried ear for a watch fob, boy, you go ahead an' get suspicious, hear?"

"I'll do that, Hands. Indeed I will." Smiling, Longarm left the barn and headed back toward town.

He had lunch at a restaurant near the courthouse where there were cloths on the tables, saucers under the cups, and even several potted plants placed around the room to make the setting more attractive. There were other places in Julesburg where he could have eaten more cheaply, but a decent meal from a decent menu in better than decent surroundings was a real treat after some of the places where he had had to eat since he left Denver.

The meal was made all the more enjoyable by the view across the room. She was blonde, tall, well if not exactly amply built, and beautiful.

Longarm had time to give the matter long and serious consideration. The conclusion he eventually reached was that the tall blonde was quite probably the most beautiful woman he had ever seen.

She was in her late twenties, he guessed. She sat in profile to him, and he could see the long, elegant line of her neck and throat under a hairstyle that was a confection of intricate curls and twists. Her nose was straight. "Patrician" came to mind when he looked at her. Her cheekbones were high. Her lips were full, her chin well defined.

He could see only her right side and was too far away to see the color of her eyes, but he imagined them to be a bright china blue.

The more he thought about it the more he realized that her figure, which he could also easily see in profile, was exactly right. Any more would have been too much. Anything less would have been too little.

She was eating alone, which Longarm considered to be one of the great wastes of all time. He was not a jealous or a possessive man. Someone surely should have been enjoying this remarkable woman's company.

She wore a simple dress, but her beauty was more than enough to make it appear as elegant as she was. There was a handbag and a plain sunbonnet on the seat of the chair across from her.

The woman had already been seated before he arrived. She finished her meal before Longarm finished his. She retrieved her bonnet and handbag and rummaged in the bag for a coin to lay on the table in payment for her meal, which had been light.

When she turned toward him as she left the restaurant he was shocked. It was all he could do to avoid staring as she passed his table.

The left side of that exquisitely lovely face had been burned.

The flesh covering most of her left cheek was a dark, mottled red, and the skin—so smooth and perfect on the right—was puckered and distorted by old scar tissue.

Her left eye—he could see in that first brief look before realization struck that her eyes were indeed a pure, crystalline blue—was nearly closed by a wrinkled fold of red scar.

The left corner of her mouth was drawn down into a permanent grimace by the effects of the old injury.

Longarm concentrated on fumbling a cheroot out of his coat pocket and lighting it so he would not appear to be deliberately looking away from her as she passed. But if he looked at her he was sure she would think he was staring rudely. If he did not, he was afraid she might think he was refusing to look at her disfigurement. As, of course, he was.

She left the restaurant, and Longarm had time to think over his coffee about what waste really meant.

When he was done he stopped at one of the town's better saloons to buy a bottle of Tom Moore for himself and a replacement jug of cheap barrel whiskey for Hands. The old fellow had not asked for anything, but the hope had been implied. Longarm did not mind.

126

He stopped at his hotel long enough to leave the bottle of good Maryland rye in his room, then went out again and headed toward the south end of town and the Simmons Express Company office.

He found Hands cleaning one of the stalls in the rear of the barn and delivered the whiskey. The old man seemed delighted and immediately pulled the cork. "Join me in a snort?"

Longarm shook his head. "I just finished lunch." He would have thoroughly enjoyed a nip of the Tom Moore and should have thought of that before he left the bottle behind, but he wanted no more of Hand's noxious tipple.

"Miz Simmons is here now," Hands volunteered. "I tol' her you'd be by."

"Thanks."

Longarm went back to the front of the barn to the former tack room and knocked.

"Come." The voice was young and almost musically rich in tone. He was surprised. He had not known what he expected, but that was definitely the voice of a lady, not just a woman.

He opened the door.

And stopped in it.

Mrs. Jennifer Simmons was the tall, blonde, once-beautiful woman he had seen not more than half an hour ago in the restaurant.

At the moment she had her eyes directed downward, poring intently over a sheaf of papers on her desk. She seemed to be giving her full attention to the paperwork even though she had just acknowledged his arrival.

That struck him as odd for a moment. Then he realized the truth.

Her evident distraction was a device she had developed, perhaps consciously or possibly without her own realization, to keep herself from having to observe the reaction visitors would have when they saw that horribly contorted left side of her face.

He felt a pang of sympathy for her when he realized what she was doing. It made her seem so vulnerable. And it occurred to him that over the years since she was burned it might well have been her feelings that had suffered the greatest damage from that accident.

Once the shock of discovery was ended, he was able to steel himself against any displays of discomfort.

"Mrs. Simmons?"

"Yes." She looked up, meeting his eyes for the first time. The right side of her face, seen full on, was still heart-breakingly lovely.

Longarm introduced himself and took the seat she offered, the same one he had occupied earlier when he was talking with Hands.

"I have already heard a great deal about you, Marshal," she said. "Among other things, I have heard that you smoke. Please feel free to do so if you wish." The voice as well as the now-ruined beauty showed breeding and culture.

Longarm could not help wondering how a woman like this had ever come to be operating a piss-ant little stage line way the hell and gone out on the plains.

On an impulse, he asked her.

Mrs. Simmons looked surprised for a moment. Then she smiled. The expression had a curious effect. The right side of her mouth curled into a pretty, dimpled smile. The left remained molded in its permanent frown. Longarm was reminded fleetingly of a poster he had seen once in the lobby of a Kansas City theater, a stark black-and-white drawing that he was told was supposed to represent the dramatic arts. It too had been half smile and half frown.

"Are you always so bold, Marshal?"

He smiled at her. "It's a fault, I'm sure. I have lots of those." He was quickly becoming accustomed to her appearance. He was able to look at her now without feeling awkward about it. Relaxing, he reached inside his coat and withdrew a cheroot. He bit off the tip, spat the speck of twisted tobacco into his palm, and lighted the smoke.

"I would offer you a drink, Marshal, but Alan's bottle seems to be empty."

"Alan, ma'am?"

She smiled again. The expression seemed less odd the second time. "Hands," she explained. "His real name is Alan Dorn, but he insists on calling himself Hands."

Longarm grinned. "I think that bottle's supposed to be a secret, ma'am."

"Of course it is, but I trust you won't tell on me, Marshal."

"Your secret is safe with me, ma'am."

"Must we be so formal, Marshal? My given name is Jennifer. You are welcome to use it."

"My friends call me Longarm, Jennifer."

"Very well, Longarm." She relaxed in her chair. Until she did, Longarm had not realized how much tension there was in the set of her shoulders and the stiff way she held her head. She smiled again. "You asked how I came to be here." The right side of her face twisted, then returned to a smile. "Fate, Longarm." She sighed. "The truth is that as a girl I was, shall we say, an embarrassment to my family. They

129

occupied a highly . . . social conscious position. I was not an asset. My late husband was from a once prominent family with an acceptable name and background. A marriage was arranged and a sizeable dowry paid. Alas the gentleman gambled. When the dowry was gone it was suggested that he take me elsewhere, which he did. He . . . we, I suppose I should say, although I hardly understand the logic of why . . . we engaged in one business venture after another. This happened to be the last. When my husband died I had only two choices. One, to return East to my family, was unacceptable. This is the other." She spread her hands and smiled again. Her tone of voice had been matter-of-fact, but Longarm thought he could see a great deal of pain in her eyes while she spoke.

"Are you always so bold, madam?" he asked.

She stiffened for a moment. Then, remembering where she had heard that same question so recently, she laughed. "Remind me to send a thank-you note to your superiors, Longarm. I like you."

"Thank you, Jennifer. If you wish, I can make some suggestions about what you might say in your note."

She laughed again. "I shall think about that, and let you know if I accept your offer. Now, what was it you wanted to ask me?"

"Isn't that obvious, ma'am? I came here to find out if you've been robbing your own stages, of course." He was smiling pleasantly when he said it.

"You are not only a likeable man, Marshal Long, you are a clever one as well. You disarm me with your smile, but I think your question is quite a serious one. And perfectly logical as well. My answer, if I may take your question as seriously as you truly meant it, will be to give you complete access to my records here and to both my personal and corporate bank accounts. Will that help?"

Son of a bitch, Longarm thought. The woman hadn't only been a beauty. She was smart too.

"It would be a help, but . . ."

"But, of course," she finished for him, "if I so freely offer the information, it is apparent that I have nothing to hide. Nothing, that is, that would be within your reach locally. Is that it?"

"I'm afraid so, Jennifer."

She smiled. "As long as you catch the thieves, I shall be well satisfied, and I shall take no umbrage at any line of questioning you find appropriate."

"Why, thank you, Jennifer. I doubt you know how unusual that is, and I do appreciate it."

"Believe me, Longarm, it is we who appreciate your help. We quite frankly are at the end of our wits over this problem. I know Royce has already told you about the loss of our insurance coverage. Without that or some other means to assure financial liability we may well lose our contract with the United States Post Office. And frankly, Longarm, we would not be able to continue operations without that contract."

"I see," he said.

"Now, what more can I tell you?"

"Everything would be nice," he said.

"Very well. Everything it shall be, sir."

She leaned forward in her chair and began to shuffle through the papers on the desk before her. She took out one and handed it to him, then another.

Before the afternoon was done, Longarm knew more than he had ever really wanted to know about the costs and the operations of a small stage line.

About the only thing he did not know was how the

131

robbers were getting their information.

And that, of course, was the only thing he genuinely wanted to learn about running a stage service.

Chapter 11

Longarm slouched back in the hard chair and rubbed his eyes. He was tired and hungry and wished like hell he had brought that bottle of Tom Moore with him instead of leaving it at the hotel.

It was sometime well after dark. They had been going through Jennifer Simmons's papers by lamplight for nearly an hour. The return leg stage from Holyoke had long since reported in, and both Royce Hapwell and Hands had probably had time to finish their suppers and be well on the way to a good drunk by now. Longarm almost wished he was with them.

"I think that covers everything I can think of," Mrs. Simmons said. She shoved the last of the papers into a pile on her desk and used the edges of her palms to neaten them into a thick, tidy stack.

"It should," Longarm said.

Jennifer looked away from him. He thought he saw her color slightly. "I'm sorry," she said. "Sometimes my enthusiasm runneth over."

"You really do enjoy business, don't you?"

She nodded. "It is a challenge. I enjoy challenge."

Which, he thought, was probably quite true. But only a partial truth. It had been apparent for some time that she was bringing out a great deal of material that could have had no bearing whatsoever on matters that would interest anyone but an accountant. He had no idea why, but he was certain she had been doing it, and doing it quite deliberately.

She shifted in her chair so that her right side, the good side, was toward him. This time he was certain she was blushing when she suggested, "I have kept you from your supper. Could I make amends by offering you dinner? Please?" She said it hesitantly, as if she fully expected to be refused. As if she dared not hope for an acceptance.

"It would be a pleasure, Jennifer," he said.

She cut her eyes sideways toward him, smiling and grateful, very careful still not to show him the disfigured side of her face, even though he had been with her for the entire afternoon.

In fact, he realized, he had been with her so much, had become so accustomed to the sight, that it no longer seemed so shocking or even so ugly as it had. The realization was in itself something of a shock.

She looked to be very pleased with his answer. Then her expression changed to one of dismay. Her eyes went wide. After a moment she laughed and told on herself. "I shall have to invite you to a restaurant as my guest, Longarm. I am not domestic. I never learned."

"The treat will be the company, not the meal, regardless," he said gallantly.

Jennifer Simmons blushed furiously.

"One thing, though," he said.

"Yes?" She looked a bit worried.

"Since we'll be dining in public, we'll let the government pay for our dinners." This was not, strictly speaking, a proper expense. But he had just spent the afternoon going over her books. He knew the financial shape she was in. And, damn it, if Billy disallowed this one, why, he would just pay for the damn meals himself.

"I couldn't possibly..."

"I insist," he said. He stood and offered her his arm. She hesitated for less than a heartbeat, then smiled and nodded her assent. She hurried to grab up her handbag and bonnet and to lay her fingertips lightly in the crook of the gentleman's arm.

Longarm opened the low gate in the picket fence and held it for her, closing it behind them and then returning to her side. He was laughing, as he had been doing for much of the evening. Jennifer had never said or so much as hinted at where she had been reared, but her stories about her childhood were gay and light and amusing. She was good company.

And, he thought, she had displayed considerable relish when several women, obviously locals, had come into the establishment and seen her in the company of a tall, good-looking stranger. She had tried to conceal her pleasure, but only a blind man would have been able to miss the satisfied way she preened and giggled. Longarm found himself being glad that he had been able to give her that pleasure, and he had had to remind himself sternly that in spite of everything she still was a suspect in this case.

He led her onto the front porch of her small house and held the door open for her.

She stopped in the doorway, her right side toward

him, and he noticed that she was wringing her hands together in a display of nervousness. "Would you . . . that is . . . would you care to . . . come inside?"

"If it wouldn't be an imposition."

"No," she said quickly. "I . . . haven't anything to drink. But I could steep some tea. Would you like a cup of tea?"

"Very much." The lie slid out smooth and easy. Damn it. *Damn* it. He was beginning to like this woman. And it no longer had anything to do with feeling sorry for her. She honestly was a pleasure to be with.

She smiled and led the way inside the house.

No lamp had been left burning. She found matches while Longarm waited near the door—better that than falling all over her furniture—and lighted a small lamp in a far corner of the front parlor. There were other lamps in the room, but she blew the match out and left the others alone. "I shall be back in a moment. Make yourself comfortable, Longarm."

"All right." He removed his Stetson and hung it on an ornate gilt hook beside the door. Jennifer disappeared into the back of the house, and he could hear the clang of an iron door being opened. She would be building a fire in the stove and putting water on for the tea he did not really want.

Longarm helped himself to a seat on the right end of the sofa. That would allow Jennifer to sit with her good side toward him and would keep her out of the light. He thought she would find that more comfortable.

She was back shortly. "It won't take long," she said.

"No hurry." He meant it. He was in no hurry at all to end the evening.

He reached inside his coat for a cigar, then realized there were no ashtrays visible in the fluffy, feminine parlor. He put the cheroot away again.

"Please. Go ahead," she said. "I'll bring something."

She went back to the kitchen and returned with a small china bowl that was never intended for such crude use. When she leaned over him to place the bowl on the table at his side, he could see the silken texture of her fine skin and smell the delicate scent of her powder.

From that angle, and so very close, she was once again the most beautiful woman he had ever seen.

Without thinking about it, he reached up and lightly touched the softness of her cheek.

Jennifer broke into tears. Without warning she broke down and began to sob. She turned and raced away into the kitchen.

Longarm sat awkwardly for several minutes. Then he followed her.

The kitchen was dark except for a faint dance of flame that licked at the cast iron inside the firebox of her stove.

He struck a match and held it up.

"No!" She was still crying. "Please don't."

He extinguished the match, pressed the burnt head between his thumb and forefinger to make sure it was out, and dropped the spent match into his pocket. He made his way toward her slowly, moving toward the place where her voice had been.

He groped his way along, not wanting to walk into anything in the dark. His hand found her shoulder. She was trembling.

He wrapped his arms around her and pulled her to him.

137

She resisted for a moment. Then, with a sob of bitter anguish, she yielded and came inside the circle of his arms.

She pressed herself against his chest. Her face—so beautiful, so ugly—nestled against his throat.

Longarm cupped her chin in his hand and lifted, tilting her head back.

He bent and found her lips. They were tight with resistance at first. Then she opened her mouth and accepted his kiss, was kissing him back with a fierce passion.

He had quite forgotten about her disfigurement now. She was a woman. And she was beautiful.

She led him to the bedroom, her arm flung protectively—or possessively—around his waist. Longarm let her lead the way in the house that was familiar to her. He did not suggest that they light a lamp. She would be more comfortable in the darkness.

They found the softness of the bed by feel and separated for a moment. He could hear the faint rustle of cloth as she undressed.

Longarm pulled his clothes off quickly. Habit made him retain his gunbelt and hang the heavy Colt on the headboard post where he could reach it if need be. The thought, uncharitable though it might be, came to him that she was still a suspect in the case. He did not dare make any assumptions in her favor, however unfair that might be.

She came into his arms again, and all such thoughts were swept away.

The slim elegance of her bare flesh pressed cool and sleek against his skin, and for that moment he was aware of nothing but the feel of her, the tastes and the textures.

He examined that long, lovely body by touch, beginning at her chin cupped in his hand, then down the narrow column of her throat. He could feel her pulse racing there, matching the quickened speed of her breath.

Jennifer quivered when he touched her right breast. It was firm and delightfully rounded. As he had noticed before, before he even knew her, it was ample in size without being overlarge, in perfect proportion to the rest of her. Just right.

He found a tiny, firmly engorged nipple and rolled it lightly between his thumb and middle finger, then ran his palm slowly down over the flat planes of her belly to tangle his fingers in a scant patch of silken hair at her vee.

Jennifer moaned and canted her hips up and forward to accommodate him. Her hands crept slowly between them.

Longarm's erection was already pressing against her stomach. She found it and fondled it with both hands, her breath sharply indrawn when she felt the length of him.

She pulled away from his kiss and sank slowly to her knees, running the tip of her tongue across his chest as she drifted downward. Her tongue twisted and curled through the hair on his chest and lapped briefly at each of his nipples, then down across his belly. The tip darted into his navel and then went lower still.

She was on her knees now. She still held him gently in her hands. Then, eagerly, she leaned forward. She took him between her lips and drew him into the sweet heat of her mouth.

Longarm braced his feet apart and stroked the back

of her head with his hands. She seemed in no hurry. Neither was he.

After a time she withdrew from him and rocked back onto her heels. He cupped his hand under her chin again and raised her up.

He bent and placed one arm behind her knees, then scooped her up into his arms. She shivered with pleasure at his strength and began to lick what she could reach of his chest.

Quickly he found the edge of the bed and laid her onto it, then joined her, pressing his hard frame against her much softer, yielding body.

He found her with his fingertips and dipped slowly inside, then just as slowly pulled back and began to manipulate the tiny button of her pleasure. He pulled first one nipple and then the other into his mouth and sucked on them while he stroked her.

Within moments Jennifer's hips began to pulse and move with his touch. She arched her back and pressed upward against him. He accepted the cue and fingered her harder and faster.

Once she tried to pull him onto her, but he resisted, continuing as he had been until he felt the shudders and the convulsive contractions of her climax.

He let her relax for a moment then, leaving her breasts to hold her against him until she had come down from the heights where he had taken her.

Only then did he lift himself over her and lie on top of her.

Her body had been cool when they began. Now her flesh was warm and lightly filmed with perspiration.

He was still achingly erect. He lifted himself away from her, and she reached between their bodies to find and to guide him while she opened herself wider for his entry.

When Longarm slid into her she sighed and wrapped her arms and those long, sleek legs tight around him, drawing him deeper into her until he was fully socketed within the wet heat of her.

He lay motionless for a bit, allowing her to adjust to his presence, then began to stroke slowly with a shallow rocking motion.

Her response was quick. She began to pump her hips to meet him. Only then did he lengthen his strokes and increase their frequency. He allowed her to build again, matching her efforts with his own.

Only at the last, when both of them were grunting with the effort of their coupling, when their sweat-slick bellies were slapping together loudly, did he permit himself free rein and drive hard and fast into her.

Jennifer climaxed seconds before his explosion. He felt her arms and legs clutch at him with a frantic strength and felt the tight, demanding pull of her convulsing sex around the base of his cock.

Then he shuddered and spewed out a hot rush of fluid, stiffening as he did so and then, spent, collapsing onto her.

They lay quiet for a time, exhausted, neither moving or wanting to move.

Then Jennifer reached up to stroke his temple and cheek lightly with her fingertips.

When Longarm tried to withdraw and remove his weight from her, she held him close, not wanting him to go.

Later she rolled him off her and pressed down on his chest, commanding him to stay there. Not knowing

141

what she wanted, but willing for the moment to go along with it, he did as she wished.

She sat up beside him. It was too dark for him to see what she was doing. After a bit he heard the faint, metallic ting of pins dropping to a hardwood floor. When she bent over him again he could feel the feather touch of her unpinned hair tickling his belly. And then lower.

She took him into her mouth again and sucked the spent juices from him, cleaning and at the same time arousing him.

"You don't have to do that," he said.

She pulled away. "I want to."

She engulfed him again, and he stroked the back of her head. He smiled in the dark and trailed his hand lightly down the smooth contours of her back to rest at an impossibly narrow waist.

He let her do the work of it, willing himself to remain motionless.

In an amazingly short time he could feel deep in his groin the rise of pressure, the growing, relentless surge of pleasure, increasing and then again until the pressures were too great to contain, the pleasures too much to delay.

He spurted forth again with a loud groan, and Jennifer held him deep and warm inside her while she drained the last possible drops from him.

When she finally released him and sat up, she sighed.

He did not have to ask her how it had been for her. And he knew damn good and well how it had been for him.

He pulled her down to nuzzle against his shoulder and absently ran his palm up and down the silky skin.

He had not yet seen her body, and quite possibly never would, but it occurred to him that she felt like total, unmarred perfection everywhere except in that one area that was always on public display.

On an impulse he kissed her forehead, not realizing until afterward that he had kissed the left side of her forehead and not caring even then, and detached himself from her arms.

"You're leaving?" she asked quickly.

He chuckled softly. "Only if you want me to."

"No. I don't."

"Good," he said. "Because I don't want to go. If you don't mind, I'd enjoy a cigar. And then, well, we'll see what happens then."

Jennifer sighed with joy and rolled onto her back.

In the flare of the match, before he used it to light his cheroot, Longarm confirmed what he had already believed.

Her body was utter perfection.

She lay with the left side of her face pressed into a feather pillow, and from this view she was total beauty from hair to toenails.

He smiled and shook the match out, then drew deeply on the smoke from the cheroot.

He was quite content when he lay back down beside her.

Chapter 12

Longarm walked with her to the company barn early Monday morning. He had spent Saturday night, all day Sunday, and most of Sunday night with her, nearly all of that time in bed, although several times she had had to get dressed to go out for food. She had been telling him the truth when she said she was not domestic. When he arrived she had not had a thing in her kitchen except for tea leaves and sugar. And on Sunday they had not even been able to have tea until she had been out the first time. She had put water on to boil Saturday night and then forgot about it, and now the kettle was ruined from remaining on the stove after the water boiled away.

Longarm would have been glad to run the errands for her, but her reputation would have suffered had he been seen coming and going.

This morning he had slipped out before dawn to return to his hotel for a quick bath and a change of shirt and balbriggans.

He felt good now, thoroughly drained, thoroughly refreshed.

And he was pleased that over the weekend Jennifer had lost her shyness about letting him see her. That had been inescapable come Sunday morning, and she had not been willing for him to leave. She had seemed proud to be seen with him at breakfast too. They had met at the restaurant to insure against wagging tongues and now were able to walk openly together to the Simmons Company barn.

She walked on his left by habit, presenting her good side to him, although probably even she realized by now that he was no longer consciously aware of her burn scars.

Over the weekend she had told him that she was scarred when as a toddler she tipped over a burning lamp and ignited spilt whale oil on her face and clothing. Longarm had not really thought about the scars since then.

Now it was time for him to get back to business.

"Do you know if there's any valuable freight this trip?" he asked. It was the first time either of them had mentioned the robberies or anything relating to them since they reached her house on Saturday evening.

"Not that I would know of," she said. "But then I normally would not. I very seldom know in advance how many passengers will be wanting to travel or what manner of freight we may be asked to carry."

"What about the things that came in on Saturday?" he asked.

"Even before the robberies began, we rarely had anything delivered on Saturdays for Monday shipment. I assume that has to do with the isolation and the condition of our barn. If anyone wanted to come in and pilfer over the weekend they easily could. So we never have gotten much delivered on Saturdays, and never anything of value. Now, as everyone is aware of the robberies, there is nothing at all brought in before the coach is ready to leave." She sighed. "And frankly, dear, there is little enough brought in then. As you may have already gathered from my books, our freight receipts have dropped away to practically nothing. If it were not for the mail contract I would no longer be in business here."

Longarm found himself wanting to assure her that nothing would disrupt the mail contract, that he would protect her. It was a damned unprofessional attitude, and it annoyed him, but it was also undeniably the truth. The impulse was there whether he welcomed it or not.

Hands and Royce Hapwell and a slender, bespectacled little man Longarm had never seen before were already at work when Longarm and Jennifer arrived. The coach had been pulled into the yard in front of the barn, and the wheelers were already harnessed and in hitch. Hands and Hapwell were working on the leaders while the third man carried several small bundles from the office and put them into the luggage boot.

There were no passengers in sight, but the stage was not scheduled to depart for another half hour.

"Good morning," Jennifer said brightly, directing the greeting to no one in particular.

Hapwell smiled at her and went on with what he was doing. Hands ignored her. He had the bleary eyes and shaking hands of a man not yet recovered from a rip-roarer of a hangover. Only the third man really responded. He closed and latched the lid of the luggage boot and came hurrying toward her with both hands extended and searching for hers.

"Where have you been all weekend, Jenny? I've been worried quite sick about you. I asked for you at supper last night, and they said you hadn't been in all *day*." He sounded quite distressed. And, Longarm thought, more than a little bit prissy.

Or was that jealousy? Longarm asked himself. A reaction like that was not like him. But the truth was that he was not really sure.

For whatever reason, he knew good and well that he did not like this little fool who was wringing Jennifer's hands now.

The man was small-boned and soft. His hands were no harder or more masculine than Jennifer's, and his glasses gave him an owlish, goggle-eyed look. He was hatless and Longarm could see that his hairline was receding from both front and rear, although he was probably not yet out of his twenties.

He and Jennifer seemed to be very well acquainted, though. She was making no effort to hide her scars from him. She even seemed pleased to see him, and her tone of voice was patient and kind when she lied away her weekend disappearance.

When she was done with her explanations—whatever they were; Longarm had not really been listening to the words, only to the tone—she turned and introduced them.

"Deputy Marshal Custis Long, I should like you to meet my dear friend and neighbor, Jonathan Truesdell. Jonathan, Marshal Long." She was smiling.

Truesdell offered his hand, so Longarm shook it. He even managed to avoid, somehow, being the kind of show-off son of a bitch he detested; he shook the little prick's hand lightly and did not crush the soft

148

hand in his own powerful grip. But it took some will-power for him to do it.

"My pleasure, Deputy," Truesdell said.

"The same," Longarm muttered, although it was a lie.

Jonathan took Jennifer by the elbow and led her off to the side, nattering at her in a high, nasal voice that sounded close to a whine. Longarm damn sure was not interested in listening. He went over and helped Hapwell and Hands finish making up the four-horse hitch.

On Saturday he had asked Jennifer why the Simmons line used worn-out horses for their hitches instead of the much more common and durable mules usually found pulling freight or long-haul coaches. Her answer had been simple—expense. It was, how-ever, a pleasure to work with horses instead of the much less tractable mules.

For the first time since last spring there was a crisp, refreshing nip in the air, and the horses seemed to enjoy it as much as Longarm did. They were fresh after three full days of rest, and they frisked slightly and tossed their heads as they were fitted with collars and led into the hitch in front of the wheelers.

"Will you be ridin' shotgun?" Hapwell asked when he was ready with everything except any last minute passengers.

"I don't know yet," Longarm told him. "It de-pends."

"Well, let me know before I get outa shouting dis-tance." Hapwell pulled a twist of tobacco from his back pocket and offered it. Longarm declined, and Hapwell bit off a chew for himself.

The departure time came and went. Ten minutes

after the coach should have pulled out, Jennifer walked sadly over to them. "You might as well leave now, Royce." A panicky expression widened her eyes and she asked, "The mail pouch was delivered this morning, wasn't it?"

"Yes'm," Hapwell assured her. "Right on time."

She looked relieved.

Hapwell climbed into the driving box and released his brake. "Hyup, now," he called. "Git on, boys."

The horses twitched their ears and leaned into their collars. Slowly at first and then with a will they brought the coach smoothly into motion and set themselves into a smooth, ground-covering trot. With so little load behind them they should be able to hold that pace comfortably until Hapwell stopped for his solitary lunch down at the stock tank.

Hands mumbled something and started off toward town. Probably for a hair of the dog, Longarm thought. He looked like he needed something to get his heart started this morning.

Longarm followed Jennifer into the office.

"Where's your friend?" he asked as he looked around and realized they were alone. Before she could answer he took her by the shoulders and swung her around to face him. He bent and kissed her, which brought a pleased reaction. When he released her, her face was flushed and she looked like she was ready to go back to bed, although she did not look a bit tired.

"Whew!" she breathed.

Longarm helped himself to a seat and pulled out a cheroot. One of these days he was going to have to cut down on the smoking, but *damn* it tasted good. So did Jennifer, for that matter, and he had no intention of cutting down on her as long as he was in the neighborhood.

She sat in the swivel chair behind the desk and said, "You asked about Jonathan?"

Longarm nodded. "I know from your books that he isn't an employee, but he sure acts like one."

Jennifer blushed. "Jonathan is our high-school teacher. The school is right over there." She pointed in the general direction of Julesburg. Longarm remembered having seen the school building the first time he walked out here.

"Uh-huh," Longarm said. "That explains everything, it does. The man's a high-school teacher, so he just naturally comes around to help you get the stage off."

She blushed again. "I think . . . well, I believe that Jonathan is fond of me. Although I certainly cannot imagine why."

Longarm laughed. "Can't imagine why?"

She touched the side of her face.

"Idiot woman," Longarm said. He got up and leaned across the table to kiss her again. "That's why. Because you are one hell of a female person. Including the way you look."

For a moment pain crossed her face. "I have heard the expression, dear. Put a bag over her head and she wouldn't be half bad in bed." She frowned. "I have heard that behind my back on more than one occasion, I assure you."

Longarm shrugged. "Which only proves that women don't have a corner on being fools. Now me, lady, the only reason I'd kick you outa bed is because there might be more thrashing room on the floor." He grinned and kissed her again, this time deliberately planting it on her ugly, ravaged left cheek. Its appearance had totally ceased to bother him. He was only aware of the quality of the woman who was beneath it.

151

Jennifer blushed again and deliberately changed the subject. "Anyway," she said, "Jonathan does seem to have a feeling for me. He comes over nearly every morning we have a coach leaving and helps until it is time for him to go to class. And he is here every evening we have the coach returning except on Saturdays. Saturdays he has off and he always goes down to Sterling to see his sister, so he can't be here then. He was quite apologetic about that for the longest time," she said with a laugh.

"Are you two close?" It was a question he should not have asked, and he knew it, but he had not been able to keep it from coming out. This woman seemed to have a hold on him.

"Dear! *Please!* Jonathan?" She giggled, then became more serious. "Really, darling, I may be ugly but I am not completely foolish. You seem genuinely to like me. And it is not that you do so in spite of my . . . handicap. You do so because, I believe, you truly like me."

"I can attest to that, ma'am," Longarm said solemnly.

"Jonathan, poor man, feels sorry for me. Which is quite all right, of course. There are many who do. I understand that. But in Jonathan's case . . . Oh, how can I put this so that you will understand? My physical ugliness makes him feel . . . superior. I believe I am supposed to be grateful that he is willing to overlook my appearance. Probably he expects that eventually I will be so overwhelmed with gratitude that I will fall into his bed. And the poor man is such a . . . a fool that he probably believes that is the only way he will ever be able to have a woman who is not, shall we say, public property." She shrugged. "I feel sorry

152

for *him*, really. But he can be such a likeable little imp that I enjoy his company too." She sighed. "And the truth is, dear, until you came along, I truly have been lonely. Jonathan's company has been preferable to no company at all."

Longarm did not feel sorry for her, exactly, but his heart did go out to her after that confession of loneliness.

He felt an unexpected surge of desire for her and stood, crushing his cheroot out in the cracked remnants of a dish set on the desk for that purpose. "Do you think it will be a spell before Hands gets back?"

"Probably. Why?"

"I was just thinking, ma'am. This here barn has a loft to it."

"Yes?"

"And likely there's hay up in that loft?"

"Of course." She made a face. "Horribly expensive hay, too."

"Exactly," Longarm said with satisfaction.

"So?"

He grinned at her and winked. "Ever hear the expression 'having a roll in the hay'?"

Jennifer threw her head back and laughed. "Have you no limits, dear?"

"Well, I don't know. But I'm sure willing to try and find out."

She took his hand and led the way to the ladder into the hayloft.

Chapter 13

Longarm and Jenny had lunch together at another of Julesburg's restaurants, and afterward they parted.

"Won't you come back with me?" Jennifer asked. "I could send Hands on an errand." She smiled. "A very long errand."

"You tempt me. I swear you do," Longarm told her. "But I have work to do."

She brightened. "Do you have something in mind to stop the robberies?"

Longarm shook his head. "No, I'm afraid not. But I have to check in with the postmaster. After all, he's the one who filed the report and brought me onto the case. I have to talk to him and to the sheriff here."

He was not exactly telling her the truth. He had already spoken with both men. All of the checking in that needed to be done had already been accomplished.

But, damn it, as much as he was coming to like this woman—and he was, much more than he wanted to—she remained a suspect.

And not for Jennifer Simmons, not for anyone, would he neglect his duty.

If Jennifer turned out to be the one who was feeding

information to the robbers, he would put the cuffs on her graceful, loving hands. It would damn near break his heart if he had to do that, but he would.

He squeezed her hand—wishing he could give her a kiss instead, but they were on a public street—and let her go alone back to the barn.

He knew what she would do there for the rest of the afternoon.

There was absolutely no work to be done there now. None at all until the coach returned from Holyoke tomorrow evening. But she would sit there behind that desk, poring over and over again those same papers she had shown him on Saturday. Looking, worrying, trying to find some measure of hope that her business would not fail.

Unless, of course, she was sitting there daydreaming, waiting for the time when the business finally would fail and dreaming about where she might go and how she might spend the money she had caused to be stolen from her passengers and shippers before the loss of insurance coverage and loss of customers gave her the excuse she needed to leave Julesburg without arousing suspicion.

Longarm did not really believe that that was the case with Jennifer Simmons. But he had to consider the possibility.

He sighed and headed in the other direction from the one Jennifer had taken.

He had not totally lied to her. He did need to see the postmaster again, and he needed to send a telegraph message to Denver.

This was Monday. The coach would make the return leg from Holyoke on Tuesday. Wednesday morning it would start south again.

Yes, Longarm thought as he walked. There was plenty of time to work it all out.

As he walked, beginning to feel better about things now that he had something firmly in mind, he stuck his hands into his trousers pockets and began to whistle.

Anyone who observed him would have thought he did not have a care in the world.

And, except for one remote possibility, he did not.

Wednesday morning, as he had for the past several mornings, Longarm had breakfast in public with Jennifer after first slipping out of her house before dawn and then openly returning to walk with her to the restaurant.

When they were done with their meal, Longarm excused himself long enough to go up to his hotel room and get his rifle. Then they walked together to the barn.

"Is something wrong, dear?"

He shook his head. "Just a hunch. In case I need to ride with Royce this morning. Does it make you nervous?"

"No, not really. I just haven't seen you with a gun before."

He raised an eyebrow and pointed toward the butt of the Colt that always rode just to the left of his belt buckle ready for an instant draw.

Jennifer laughed and squeezed his arm. "That one is so much a part of you, I quite forget about it. But I shall miss it, dear, when it is no longer hanging on my bedpost."

Longarm looked around uncomfortably, but there was no one within hearing. He had begun to worry a

157

great deal about this woman's reputation.

Jennifer sighed happily. "Did you know, dear, that you are more of a gentleman than any of those I left behind?"

They came in sight of the barn, and Jennifer looked even happier. "Look."

Longarm looked. In addition to the expected coach in front of the old structure, there were also two light driving rigs parked there, and a saddle horse was tied at the rail. "Busy," he said.

"I knew this morning it was going to be a good day," Jennifer said.

"How'd you know?"

She gave him a bawdy wink and made a loud purring sound.

"Oh," he said. "That."

There were three passengers waiting for the departure of the southbound stage that morning, three men from whom Jennifer gladly accepted cash payment for their fares.

Longarm helped Hands and Hapwell with the harnessing while Jonathan Truesdell assisted the passengers with loading their luggage into the rack at the rear of the coach.

The passengers were a mixed bag. One was seedy and aging, with the burst blood vessels of a heavy drinker speckling his nose. His luggage consisted of a very small carpetbag and a large sample case. Whatever he was selling, Longarm hoped it was not whiskey, or his profits would be gone before they were made. The next man to board the coach was pink-cheeked and balding, slightly pudgy of build but not soft. He too was several years past his prime, though he was not as old as the drummer. The third man was taller and almost as prissy in appearance as Truesdell was.

They all crawled into the coach and settled themselves, the lean, prissy fellow arguing with the drummer over which of them should have a front-facing seat and which should be required to ride backward. The drummer lost out and grumpily accepted the poorer seat.

"Do you have the mail pouch?" Jennifer asked as Hapwell climbed into the box and took up the lines.

"I do, Miz Jenny. Registered today."

"Really?"

Hapwell nodded. "Heavy sumbuck, too."

She gave Longarm a worried look, but he shook his head.

Hapwell released his brake but waited a moment before he put the team into motion. "Won't be riding along, Marshal?"

"Naw," Longarm said. He turned his head and spat. "Not worth it today, I wouldn't reckon."

Behind them the two rigs that had brought the passengers from town were turned away by their drivers. They set out at a brisk jog toward the business district.

"I think..." Hapwell began.

"Look, man," Longarm snapped, "nobody's told Mrs. Simmons about anything valuable going today. So don't worry about it."

Hapwell looked like he wanted to argue the point, but Jennifer was looking relieved to hear that Longarm would not be going with the stage, and he might have seen that. He was still frowning, but he shut up and gave them a curt nod goodbye. He spoke to his team and put them into a walk, then a slow trot. They had more weight to pull now and likely would need a fairly long rest at the nooning. They might be late getting into Holyoke as it was, so there was no more time to waste.

Jonathan Truesdell called a brief goodbye to Jennifer and ignored Longarm. Apparently, Longarm thought, the man was no more delighted with him than Longarm was with old Jonathan.

"Let's go inside, dear," Jennifer suggested.

"Sure." Longarm went with her, but when they were behind the closed office door he did not take her into his arms as she obviously expected. Instead he went behind the desk and borrowed a swallow of Hand's foul whiskey, then stood looking out the window toward town.

Jennifer came up beside him. "What is it, dear?"

"Nothing much. Just watching." After a moment he asked, "Why isn't your buddy going to the schoolhouse?"

She looked in the direction Longarm had been watching. She shrugged. "He lives over that way. Probably he forgot something and needs to stop at his house before he goes to school." She laughed. "Don't worry about Jonathan, dear. I understand he has never missed a day of school nor been late since he came here."

"How long's that been?" Longarm mused aloud.

"I don't recall exactly. Half a year or a little longer. I believe he came in the middle of the last term. After Mr. Perkins had his heart attack. Is it important?"

Longarm laughed. "Of course not. I'm just a curious sort, I reckon. Kinda goes with the job, you know."

Jennifer snuggled in against his side. "Kiss me?"

"Glad to." He did. "But now, if you'd excuse me, ma'am?"

160

"Where are you going?"

He grinned at her but did not answer. He picked up his rifle and went outside to where the saddle horse was tied. It had been ridden to the barn by one of the passengers, apparently, and left there.

Longarm shoved his Winchester into the empty rifle scabbard slung on the horse's saddle, then untied it and swung onto the animal.

"I don't understand," Jennifer said.

Longarm winked at her. "That, my dear, is the whole idea." He leaned down from the saddle to give her one more kiss, then reined the chunky sorrel toward the south and bumped it into a slow lope.

He left a confused and disappointed Jennifer Simmons behind him.

Chapter 14

Longarm reined the sorrel to a halt and dismounted. There were no trees or even bushes to tie the animal to, so he took the time to affix the hobbles he found in the saddlebags of the strange horse, then went through both pockets of the saddlebags to see what he had there.

There was no jerky, which he usually carried when packing for himself on the trail. Instead, though, he found a can of bully beef and two flat tins of sardines, a double handful of army issue hardtack, a can of peaches, and a telegraph key very much like the one he normally carried. He smiled at the discoveries. So far so good.

A quarter of a mile away the stage had stopped for its nooning. From where Longarm now waited, well off the road and hidden behind a series of rises in the rolling countryside, he could not see the coach. But he knew it was there.

Hapwell had said the robbers were apt to approach the stage from either east or west and that they sometimes split their party and attacked the coach from both sides at once. With no particular preference as to which side of the road he should travel on, Longarm had chosen to ride on the west simply to avoid the line of snow fencing that ran for such a distance through the bleak land.

He loosened the cinches of the borrowed saddle to give the horse relief from its hours of use, then sat in the shade provided by the sorrel's body—there was no other shade available, and the day was becoming a warm one again—and ate a light lunch of sardines and hardtack. He found it something of a pity that there was no rye whiskey in the saddlebags but was able to make do with a swallow of water from the canteen that hung over the horn of the deep-seated stock saddle. The saddle was a Frazier and, he had to admit, considerably more comfortable than his own military McClellan, but harder on the horse than the army model, which was why he chose to ride a McClellan. Better to pamper the horse than the rider was Longarm's opinion, but obviously not everyone shared that view.

He finished his meal and let the sorrel graze while he walked eastward for several hundred yards. When he neared the top of the last rise between him and the public road he hunkered down and edged slowly toward the top until he could see the windmill and water tank.

The coach was still there. Royce Hapwell was engaged in carrying buckets of water to the team, while the three passengers stood and waited. Apparently all of them had had time to finish their meals.

The drummer stood by himself near the side of the coach while the other two, the prissy-looking fellow and the balding man, stood together at the rear of the stage.

Longarm watched while Hapwell said something to them all. The drummer re-entered the coach immediately. The other two lingered outside long enough to open the luggage boot and remove a somewhat longish Gladstone bag, which the bald man carried with him into the coach. The last man closed the luggage rack and then joined the others inside.

Longarm watched. And smiled.

He backed away from the hilltop and made his way back to the waiting sorrel.

Gunshots. One, two, three of them. And then silence. The shots had come from the east. From the road.

Smiling again, Longarm turned the sorrel toward the sounds and kneed it into an easy lope. He had plenty of time.

He stopped the horse short of the top of the last rise and glanced at the sky. About two o'clock, he judged. And about midway between the noon stop and Holyoke, if he remembered correctly from the one time he had made the trip.

Just about where and when he had figured.

He edged the horse up the slope a few feet until he could comfortably see over the top without any danger of being seen from below.

As he had expected, the attention of everyone down there was on the robbery that was taking place.

Or which was supposed to be taking place.

There were six of them, easily identified as to their purpose.

Six horsemen spread out in a fan-like formation in front of the stopped coach. The six riders each had cloth sacks pulled over their heads. One of them wore a slouch hat jammed down over his hood. The others were hatless.

Royce Hapwell had already set his brake and wrapped his lines around the brake handle by the time Longarm got into a position to see. The jehu stood and raised his arms, and one of the riders, then two more, moved closer to the coach.

The lead robber yelled something, although the distance was too great for Longarm to hear what was said.

Hapwell bent, one hand held carefully in sight, and picked up the heavy, double-locked registered-mail pouch. He tossed it onto the ground a few feet from the side of the coach, and two of the mounted robbers started forward.

Without warning, flame lanced out of both side windows of the coach, and then again.

A moment later Longarm could hear the hollow thunder of the shotgun blasts as two of the men inside the coach cut loose with sawed-off double scatterguns.

The three robbers closest to the coach were cut down in that initial fusillade, and two of their horses as well. Buckshot is no respecter of horseflesh.

Hapwell threw himself to the floor of the driving box, and a frightened, edgy team tried to pull the coach forward against the drag of the brakes.

That, Longarm knew, made the coach a lousy platform for marksmanship, but someone riding on the left side of the coach was a damned good shot.

Pistol fire followed quickly behind the shotgun blasts, before any of the remaining robbers had a chance to react, and a fourth hooded bandit fell from his saddle with a .45 slug in his chest.

Longarm grinned. He had an idea of just who it was riding by the left side window. That shooting had to have come from Billy Vail, the pink-cheeked, balding "passenger" who was riding to Holyoke today.

Henry, Billy's clerk, might have some faults, but cowardice or any inclination to shirk the call of duty was not among them. The scrawny and oftentimes stuffy clerk leaned out of the right side window of the coach to snap off a string of shots at the heavy-set robber. He missed, but he must have come damn close. The robber ducked and put the spurs to his horse.

A moment later the last remaining robber, on Billy Vail's side of the stage, clutched his chest and tumbled backward out of his saddle.

Longarm nodded grimly.

It had been exactly as clean a sweep as they had hoped for.

Longarm waited a moment, letting the escaping robber line out in the direction he intended to take.

Then Longarm spurred the sorrel Billy Vail had left for him at the barn.

The horse was a good one. It leaped forward in pursuit of the fleeing man.

Longarm reined it back to slow its pace a little.

He did not want to catch the man.

Not quite yet.

The robber was running scared, but Longarm hoped he had no idea that he was being followed.

He should not realize it. That was the whole idea of the ambush the way it had been set up. As far as the man knew, the gang had been cut apart by men waiting inside the Simmons coach. And there was no way a stagecoach could hope to follow the speed or the direction of the horseman's path now.

He should have no way to guess that Longarm was riding behind him.

The man made a wide circle to the west, then swung back to the north, behind the route the coach would be taking, and crossed to the east side of the road.

He seemed to know where he was going.

He crossed the public road opposite one of the narrow paths leading off toward the east. His tiring horse jumped the line of downed snow fence and cantered on.

Longarm, relaxing now, followed. His sorrel loped easily through a gap in the fence south of the road the robber had taken.

Longarm suspected the man thought he was home free now and was heading straight for the safety of his own four walls.

That guess was confirmed half an hour later when Longarm came in sight of a sod house backed up against the eastern slope of one of the innumerable rises. Longarm pulled his sorrel to a halt and watched while the robber, no longer wearing his hood, dismounted and turned his sweating and still saddled horse into a pen in the bottom in front of the soddy.

Longarm gave the man time to get inside. He sat on the sorrel with a knee hooked over the horn of the borrowed saddle—Billy Vail's preference, even though the marshal advocated army saddles for his men— and smoked a cheroot. He wanted to give the robber time, but not too much time.

When he thought the wait had been long enough, he turned the sorrel aside and rode down into a shallow depression beside the ranch road.

Uh-huh, he thought.

It was about what he had expected to find.

A thin wire propped on low sticks ran along the north side of the earthen track.

Longarm dismounted, got the telegraph key out of his saddlebags, and hooked into the wire.

He waited. Five minutes, ten, fifteen.

There was no activity on the key.

That puzzled him.

Surely the robber would be reporting back to whoever it was who had been planning these robberies.

Or would he?

Longarm glanced at the sky.

It was mid-afternoon, three-thirty or a little shy of that time.

If Longarm's suspicions were correct, it might still be a little early for the man to be making his report.

Longarm unclipped his key from the wire and returned it to the saddlebags, then mounted and rode closer to the soddy.

He dismounted and hobbled the horse and with his Colt in hand slipped down the slope against which the low structure had been built.

He walked lightly out onto the roof. The only way in or out of the soddy was the door that was directly beneath him. The robber could not get away.

But Longarm did not want only this man. He wanted the boss too. He could afford to wait.

He bellied down on the sod roof and crawled toward the back of the place, back toward the sheet-metal stovepipe that protruded through a tin collar that ran through the thick roof. He lay with his ear against

169

the pipe—thank goodness it was a warm day and there was no fire in the stove—and waited to eavesdrop on the transmission he was sure would take place soon. A glance at his Ingersol showed the time should be about right now. He smiled while he waited. As soon as the robber began tapping out signals on his telegraph key, Longarm would be able to hear as well. And unless both of them had awfully fast hands, the deputy would be able to read both ends of the conversation.

After a while Longarm heard an odd whirring noise and then conversation.

He almost sat up away from the pipe in his surprise.

Had he misfigured it so completely? Were *both* of them inside the soddy?

And why could Longarm hear only one side of the conversation? Why could he not hear the boss's voice too?

"It's me," the robber said. He sounded weary but no longer excited.

"I got bad news. . . . Yeah, damn it, real bad. . . . Just shut up a minute an' let me tell you, will you?"

Longarm was puzzled by the odd delays while the other person was obviously speaking yet could not be heard from above.

"Just shut up, will you?" the robber repeated. "We got hit today. . . . No, damn it, I'm telling you, we got *hit!* Two of them, at the least. They tore us apart, I'm tellin' you. No warning. They was inside the coach, an' all billy-hell broke loose. . . . Shotguns, damn it. Shotguns an' pistols an', hell, maybe Gatling guns for all I know. I mean, we was doing just fine, right accordin' to plan, an' then the next thing I know there's dead men and dyin' horses everywhere I looked

170

and . . . What the fuck d'you *think* I did? I ran like hell, that's what I did. . . . No, shit, there's no way I coulda been followed. The gunmen was all inside the coach; I already *told* you that. . . . No. . . . If you say so. . . . Oh, hell, I don't know. A week maybe. I'd have to go over to Ogallala or maybe Scottsbluff to find them. . . . Yeah, I can get some more, but I think we ought to lay off for . . . I *know* that, but I think . . . I know, I know, but by damn you was wrong this time, weren't you?"

The robber sounded exasperated. And no wonder, Longarm thought. The boss, whoever it was, was not the one who had just been shot at. No wonder this man down below was having doubts about the wisdom of immediately putting another gang together with replacements for the dead men. And that was pretty obviously what was being discussed.

The two talked a little longer, mostly with the gang member complaining about the boss's desire to press on with their scheme and the boss apparently insisting that they continue. Longarm still could not hear that side of the conversation.

After a while the robber said, "All right, damn it, but I don't really like it. I, uh, I'll talk to you in a couple days then. . . . Yeah, before I leave to find some more boys. I'll talk to you before then. . . . Yeah, I will. . . . You too. . . . Yeah, goodbye."

And there was silence.

Longarm was still puzzled but it was obvious he was not going to learn anything more by waiting on the roof of the soddy. He began to make his way toward the front of the place, careful to make no noise when he moved.

A moment later he heard the door of the soddy

open, and the robber, now wearing a sweat-stained hat, came out into the yard a few feet below and in front of the deputy.

Probably going to take care of his horse, Longarm thought. It was about time, too.

Longarm stood and palmed his Colt.

"Hold it," Longarm said. "Right where you are."

The man turned, his face going pale with the shock of discovery.

He was a big man, his beard nearly white, and once there would have been a bull-like power in those thick shoulders and massive wrists and arms.

Now the years had robbed him of much of that long-ago strength. He was still big, but now he was tending to flab where once there had been layers of muscle, and his belly flowed over his belt buckle.

He might have lost much of his strength, but he had lost none of his capacity for anger. Or, if he had, then he must have been one mean son of a bitch when he was younger.

Longarm could see in the man's eyes that this fading bull of the woods had no intention of letting himself be taken, regardless of the odds against him.

He saw Longarm standing there, Colt already in hand and leveled, ready to cut him down if he moved.

Yet the aging robber did not hesitate for a moment.

As soon as he saw his target he went for it, his big hand sweeping toward the butt of an ancient Remington cap and ball revolver that rode high on his hip.

The man did not have the quick reflexes of youth, and he wore his gun in an impossibly awkward manner. Yet his raw courage and his rage were undiminished. He went for the revolver even though he surely had to know he had no chance.

"Don't!" Longarm shouted. "Damn it, don't!"

Longarm did not want to shoot. He truly did not. But he had no choice.

The old robber's hand reached the butt of the Remington and pulled it clear of the leather.

His thumb eared back on the hammer, and the barrel began to tilt upward, toward Longarm's chest.

Longarm could wait no longer.

He fired, and a heavy, flat-nosed .44-40 slug ripped into the robber's chest.

The big man staggered, but even then he refused to give it up. He fought to keep his balance and to bring the muzzle of his Remington on line with Longarm's body.

Longarm shot down into him again and then again.

The third slug took him square on the forehead and snapped his head back, dropping his hat away from a bald head fringed with near-white curls.

The lifeless body staggered backward half a pace and then toppled forward, face down in the dirt of the yard.

Longarm held his Colt at the ready and leaped to the side, revolver aimed down at the doorway, ready to send another round into whoever it was this old man had been talking to down there.

But there was only silence from within the soddy.

Whoever it was was being damned cagey. And awfully quiet.

Longarm steeled himself to go in after the son of a bitch. He reloaded the big Thunderer and came down off the roof at the ready.

Chapter 15

Longarm lay on the dirt floor of the soddy. His belly hurt like hell, all the way through to his back. He held the big Colt in his right fist, its muzzle sweeping left and right and back again in search of a target.

But he did not fire.

After a moment, more confused than ever, he came to his knees.

His free hand rubbed the sore spot on his stomach, then angrily swept aside an object on the floor in front of him.

Some son of a bitch had been fool enough to leave a spur lying on the floor there. When Longarm made his dive through the open doorway he had landed right on it. It *hurt*, damn it.

On the other hand, landing on a discarded spur was considerably better than being shot when he came through that door.

What confused him, though, was that the soddy was empty.

He had heard with his own ears the gang member talking with his boss. Not five minutes ago and in this very room. There was no other way out of the soddy.

Yet now there was no one here.

Longarm shook his head and climbed to his feet, the Colt still held at the ready. There *had* to be another person here. There had to.

But there was not.

Not in or under any of the bunks that had been used by the six gang members.

Not in any hidey-hole in the dirt walls.

Not *anywhere*.

Longarm searched the place as thoroughly as he had ever searched anything, and there was nothing to be found in or near the soddy. Nothing but clothing and food and cartons of ammunition.

And, finally . . .

Shee-oot, Longarm thought. A broad grin spread slowly over his face.

There it was, right in plain sight.

The answer to how the gang had been tipped.

Soon it would also answer the question of who had tipped them to the stage shipments. Although Longarm suspected he already knew the answer to that one.

The apparatus consisted of two wooden boxes.

He had seen the like before, although never in such an out-of-the-way setting as this.

On the bottom was a battery box, a wet-cell battery the like of which you could buy by mail order from any number of catalogs, either the whole outfit or the chemicals to produce the electricity once the first battery was exhausted.

And on top of that was another wooden box, this one with a hand crank on the side, a black metal speaker in front, and a black earpiece on a cord at the side opposite the crank.

The bastards had been using a telephone, Longarm realized.

He shook his head and almost admired whoever had come up with this system.

He had expected a telegraph key and would have been prepared for that. That he could have tapped into with his own key easily. But a telephone . . . he knew of no one this side of Denver who could have intercepted any messages being transmitted by telephone, if indeed it could be done at all. Longarm had seen Bell's invention a time or two in the past, but he damn sure did not understand how they operated.

He knew for sure there was no telephone system in Julesburg yet. Probably there was none in Sterling or Fort Morgan either. Denver's system was barely functioning with a handful of subscribers to the young service.

No wonder he had only been able to hear one side of the conversation down here. The other end of it was taking place miles away, almost certainly all the way back in Julesburg. It had to be there, because that was where the coach was loaded with its freight and passengers.

The gang had never hit the northbound run of the stage for the simple reason that there was no one down at the Holyoke end to spot the marks and tip the gang to them. There would be no spotter there and no telephone except in Julesburg.

Longarm shoved his Colt back into his holster and brushed himself off. The damn floor had been filthy, and he had wallowed around on it to no purpose whatsoever.

Still, it was somewhat better to have a cleaning bill than a hole in his gut.

He checked the soddy once more, but there was nothing else of interest in the place. When he went out he closed and latched the door behind him. Come winter, someone might well need its shelter and its supplies.

He went to the corral and got the dead outlaw's horse. Getting the big man on the horse by himself was going to be a chore, but it would have to be done.

When he bent over the body, he noticed a curious thing.

The man had been carrying a watch in his vest pocket.

The fob of that watch was a small, dark brown twist of leather.

Longarm looked at it and remembered the story old Hands had told him about Black Jack Slade, the big tough who was so hard to kill.

Could this . . . ?

Longarm shook his head.

"Naw," he said out loud. "No way. No way at *all*." He stood for a moment and stared down at the body, at the gray hair and long-ago power of those muscles. He shook his head again.

"No way," he repeated to himself. "I think."

It was hours after dark before Longarm could see the sparkle of lamplight that marked the outskirts of Julesburg.

Much of the town was already in bed and sleeping. Many if not most of the houses showed blank, dark windows.

Longarm was tired, and so was his horse. The animal carrying the gang member's body was even more exhausted.

178

But while the horses would soon be done for the day, Deputy Marshal Custis Long still had work to do.

He left the line of snow fencing he had been following and rode to the Simmons Company barn.

Old Hands was asleep on a pile of hay near the doors. He smelled of sour whiskey, and Longarm let him sleep while he put up both horses and manhandled the body of the outlaw into an empty stall. It would keep there well enough until he could get back to it, although soon the body would have to have some professional attention. Morning should be soon enough for that. The days were still warm but the nights, thank goodness, were finally beginning to cool off.

He took care of the horses, throwing hay to each of them, then left the barn without waking Hands.

He walked back out onto the prairie to the snow fence and felt along the top of it between the thin wooden slats that were designed to control the drifting of the winter snows.

The vertical slats on a snow fence were held together by twists of smooth wire, one turn between each slat, one length of doubled wire near the top of the fence and another at the bottom.

But on this fence there was a third length of wire, unpaired, untwisted, and having nothing to do with the ordinary purposes of a snow fence.

Except for the fact that this wire was for a telephone instead of a telegraph, it was very much what Longarm had expected.

He had been following the wire all the way from the outlaws' soddy down near Holyoke.

And now he would be able to follow it to the man who was behind the robberies. He was convinced that

179

it would be a man, although that was yet to be proven.

Longarm followed the fence to its end, then had to stoop and fumble in the dust to find the loose-laid wire that was strung along the ground leading toward a group of houses at the south edge of Julesburg.

He stopped once and glanced back toward the barn and tried to visualize the lay of the dark houses in front of them as if he were standing inside the barn, looking in this direction from the office window.

He nodded with grim satisfaction once he had it worked out in his mind.

After that he was able to follow the loose wire in a direct line, without hesitation.

It led beneath a low fence and to a hole in a wall at the back of a small, unpainted house on the very edge of the residential district.

Longarm left the wire then and went around to the front stoop.

He palmed his Colt before he knocked.

The house was dark, its occupant probably asleep.

Longarm waited patiently.

After a moment he could see a dim flare of fire beyond the curtains of the front window and then the stronger light of an oil lamp. He heard footsteps, and the lamp moved closer to the front door.

The door swung open, and a small, mousy, spectacled man faced Longarm.

"Yes?" He blinked and seemed not to recognize his visitor.

"May I come in, Jonathan?"

"Of course, but who . . . ?"

Jonathan Truesdell blinked again, then smiled and stood back from the door. "Deputy Long. Yes, do come in." He made a gesture of apology, fluttering his hands up and down in front of the robe he was wearing. His feet were encased in carpet slippers, and the hem of a cotton nightshirt showed under the robe. "Do come in."

Longarm stepped through the door and pulled his handcuffs from his back pocket.

"Whatever are those for?" Truesdell asked.

"We'll talk in a minute," Longarm said. "Right now, Jonathan, I need to put you under arrest."

"Under arrest? Me?"

"You got it." Longarm held out the cuffs. Truesdell ignored him.

"But, Deputy . . ."

"Come off it, Jonathan. It's over. You've been found out. Your boy down south is dead. I was listening to his end of the conversation when he talked to you this afternoon. So he won't be going to Ogallala or to Scottsbluff. There won't be another gang. You're the last one left alive now, Jonathan, so you'll be the only one of the bunch lucky enough to go to prison for it."

Truesdell blinked and smiled. "I have no idea what you are talking about, Deputy."

"If it makes you feel any better," Longarm said, "it all has to be proven in court." He shrugged. "Who knows, if you got enough money to hire a really good lawyer you might not even have to serve all that much time. It's only mail theft. There's been no murders to charge you with."

"I still have no idea what you mean, of course."

"Of course."

Truesdell set his lamp on a table near the front door and removed his glasses. He pulled a handkerchief from the pocket of his robe and meticulously cleaned his spectacles, breathing on them and polishing them

181

several times before he was satisfied that they were clean enough.

He replaced them on his nose and put the handkerchief back into his pocket.

When he withdrew his hand from the robe pocket, the barrel of Longarm's Colt flashed downward, chopping Truesdell on the wrist.

The little man cried out, and a Little Ace four-barreled derringer fell onto the floor with a loud thump.

"I'll shoot you if you insist," Longarm said, "but I'd rather not."

Truesdell looked up at the much taller and stronger deputy, and his eyes began to fill with tears. Longarm snapped the cuffs onto his wrists.

"How did you figure it out?" he asked in a small voice.

"About the telephone?"

Jonathan nodded unhappily.

"In a way you could say that I didn't," Longarm admitted. "I knew there was a wire, pretty much had to be one, but until I got inside that cabin I figured it to be a telegraph. I never figured on one of those new telephone things."

Jonathan looked a little happier after the admission.

"About the wire itself, Jonathan, well, I figured that one because of a dumb mistake you boys made."

"Nonsense," Truesdell said indignantly.

"Uh-huh," Longarm said. "Really dumb."

"That could not be," Truesdell insisted.

Longarm laughed. "Jonathan, old son, you may know an awful lot. Enough to teach high school and keep the kiddies up on all the new inventions and stuff like that. But you don't know shit about some things." He chuckled again.

"Like for instance," Longarm said, "when you put that fence up, old son, you forgot one basic thing. The winter winds here blow out of the west, Jonathan."

The man looked up at him and blinked owlishly.

"You still don't get it, do you?"

Jonathan shook his head.

"It took me a couple days to realize what was wrong about that fence, Jonathan, but then it came to me. When I was riding up here the other day there was a breeze that came up. It was my ear on one side that was getting nipped by the wind. But the snow fence was on the other side. You dumb bastards put the fence on the *downwind* side of the road, where there wasn't more need for it than udders on a bull. When I realized that, I figured there had to be some other reason for a fence to be there. And then it only seemed logical that that reason might have somethin' to do with the robberies. And what was the biggest question about them? Why, how the gang got its information about when to hit the coach. Put 'em together, and it seemed only reasonable to think that there might be a wire hidden along that dumb fence. And of course there was. I checked on it the other night."

"You didn't come and arrest me then," Jonathan said.

"Wanted to catch you all," Longarm admitted. "I wired my boss in Denver. Him and another of our boys was riding that coach today with shotguns which they kept in their luggage until they were well away from the barn, so you wouldn't see any preparations for a holdup. And if you want to know, that registered-mail bag that was on the coach today, that was empty. I asked the postmaster to ship an empty bag and hold the mail over for the next run."

Jonathan looked like he wanted to cry.

"Where's your telephone set?" Longarm asked.

Jonathan shrugged and led him to it. It was a twin of the one back in the now empty soddy.

"I was so careful," Jonathan said sadly. "I bought all my materials by mail and had them shipped to me under a different name in Sterling."

"Where you're supposed to have a sister," Longarm said.

"I do *so* have a sister there," Jonathan snapped.

"Excuse me," Longarm said. "I didn't mean to doubt your word."

"A sarcastic tone of voice is unnecessary, Deputy."

"Then I apologize for that too," Longarm said. "Well, shall we go wake the sheriff now?"

"I prefer to dress first, Deputy. I don't want to be paraded through the streets of town in my night-clothes."

"Tell you what," Longarm said, taking him by the elbow and steering him toward the door. "If you don't thump on no drums, neither will I. Then it won't be no parade."

He led the little man out into the night.

Billy and Henry would not get back until the next evening on the northbound coach leg, Longarm was thinking as they walked.

And there was no point in him running off for Denver without the boss being able to supervise things like the disposition of the sorrel horse, whoever it belonged to, or for that matter the proper disposition of Jonathan Truesdell.

Billy just might want to leave the man in the jail here to face the local charges of stage robbery before he was transferred to federal custody for mail theft and conspiracy charges.

So Longarm definitely should stay here another day or two until he could find out what Marshal Vail wanted done in this situation.

Longarm smiled and felt a certain warmth growing in his belly.

If he had to hang around Julesburg anyway, why, he might as well pass the time with a certain lady named Simmons.

He looked up toward the moon, trying to judge the hour by its passage. It was late, of course. Jennifer was bound to be in bed asleep by now. If he went calling he was sure to wake her and disturb her sleep.

But, Longarm thought with a smile, he doubted that she would mind all that much.

He sure intended to find out.

And the more he thought about that, the faster he made poor, dumb Jonathan walk. By the time they reached the jail, Longarm had him practically in a run.

Watch for

LONGARM AND THE BIG SHOOT-OUT

eighty-fifth novel in the bold
LONGARM series from Jove

coming in January!

5